Child of Grace
Irene Hannon

Steeple
Hill®

Published by Steeple Hill Books™

STEEPLE HILL BOOKS

Steeple
Hill®

Recycling programs
for this product may
not exist in your area.

ISBN-13: 978-0-373-81527-2

CHILD OF GRACE

Copyright © 2011 by Irene Hannon

www.SteepleHill.com

Printed in U.S.A.

Before I formed you in the womb I knew you,
before you were born I consecrated you.
—*Jeremiah* 1:5

To my husband, Tom—

Thank you for being my partner
on this journey called life.

Chapter One

Someone was on his beach.

Frowning, Luke Turner stopped halfway down the forty wooden steps that led to what was supposed to be a private beach on the shores of Lake Michigan. But the brim of a large, floppy hat peeked above the wide swath of tall grass between the base of the steps and the open sand. And it was low to the ground. Meaning the woman who owned it was sitting, not just pausing to admire the view while strolling by.

A definite breach of beach etiquette in this part of the world.

Stifling a sigh, he resettled the frame of his chair on his shoulder, took a sip of coffee from his mug and resumed his descent. He hadn't planned to start his visit to Pier Cove with a confrontation. He'd seen enough conflict during his past ten years as an army doctor to last a lifetime. Now that his enlistment was up, he just wanted some quiet time to reacclimatize to civilian life, complete one final mission before heading home to Atlanta and the E.R. job that awaited him, and chill.

And he'd planned to do a lot of that chilling on his private beach.

At the bottom of the steps, he stopped again to take another sip of coffee. He didn't want to make a scene. But he didn't appreciate trespassers, either. When Mark had offered him the use of his place, he'd said the house next door, which shared the beach, had been unoccupied since the owner died last fall. Luke was well within his rights to tell the woman to move on.

And maybe this would be easy. It was possible she was a vacationer who didn't know most Michigan beaches were private. If so, he could direct her to the public beach a short stroll away. Then he could enjoy this sunny Saturday morning in peaceful isolation.

Fortified by that little pep talk, he followed the narrow path through the swaying grass and stepped onto the sand.

The interloper was angled slightly away from him, seated in a beach chair, her long, shapely legs stretched in front of her, a pair of flip-flops askew in the sand beside them, as if she'd kicked them off. She was wrapped in a gaudy beach towel to ward off the morning chill Mark had warned him was common on the lakeshore even in mid-July, and her eyes were hidden behind sunglasses. Shoulder-length blond hair peeked beneath the brim of her hat, and her head was bent as she perused a book. Beside her, a thermos was stuck into the top of an overflowing beach bag, and she was juggling a mug of coffee in one hand.

In other words, she was settled in for the duration.

Bracing himself, Luke cleared his throat.

At the sound, the woman jerked toward him. The coffee sloshed out of her mug, and she yelped as the hot liquid splashed onto her skin.

Nice approach, Turner. Scare her half to death.

Luke took a step forward. "I'm sorry, I didn't mean to startle you."

Keeping a wary eye on him, she dumped the rest of her coffee into the sand and struggled out of the low-slung chair. The book slid off her lap as she rose, and the towel slipped from around her shoulders. She grabbed it…but not before he got a good look at her rounded figure.

She was pregnant.

Very pregnant.

And apparently unmarried.

Her empty ring finger was front and center as she readjusted the towel around her shoulders and clutched it in front of her.

So was the pink spot on the back of her other hand.

He took another step toward her, eyeing the burn. "Cold water will…"

She stumbled back, almost tripping over her chair on the uneven sand.

He stopped.

So did she.

But she scanned the beach, as if seeking…help?

Although he couldn't see much of her face under the large hat, and her eyes were hidden behind the glasses, he was picking up fear. Not just leftover fear from being startled, but panic almost. She seemed poised to flee. As if she thought he might become violent.

Did he look that angry?

Maybe. More than one medic had told him he was intimidating—especially when aggravated. Plus, at six-one he usually had a height advantage in any confrontation. And today he had a big one. The woman across from him couldn't be more than five-three, five-four. But he wasn't *that* mad about her being on his beach.

He forced his taut features to relax and summoned up a smile. "I'm not in the habit of…"

"This is a private beach."

At her accusatory tone, his smile faded. "Yes, it is. My beach, as a matter of fact."

Her brow wrinkled. "No, it's *my* beach. Maybe you got turned around coming through the grass."

"Maybe *you* did." He gestured toward the top of the bluff with his mug. "I'm staying at Mark Lewis's place. I got in late last night."

The creases marring her forehead deepened. "I live next door."

Luke didn't try to hide his skepticism. "Mark told me the owner of that house had died and the place was empty."

The muscles in her throat contracted as she swallowed. "The owner was my grandmother. She passed away in October. I inherited the house and moved in four months ago."

Although the woman still seemed nervous, she tipped up her chin and held her ground.

Spunky little thing.

Luke took a sip of his coffee as he mulled over her claim. Mark had been out of the country for months, on an overseas assignment for his company. It was possible he wasn't up-to-date on his neighbors. And this woman didn't appear to be lying. Nor did she seem to be any happier about sharing the beach than he was.

He surveyed the strip of sand. It was narrow, but wide. They ought to be able to make this work.

"I'll tell you what —why don't we start over, seeing that we'll be neighbors for a few weeks?" Once more he tried out a smile. Setting his mug on the sand, he moved toward her and extended his hand. "Let me introduce—"

Her grip on the towel tightened, and she took another step back.

Flummoxed, he stopped a few feet away, his hand still extended. What was with her, anyway? Maybe they hadn't gotten off on the best foot, but he hadn't done anything threatening.

As she secured the towel around her shoulders, his gaze dropped to the pink spot on her hand. It was turning red, and he suspected a blister would soon form.

He dropped his hand and nodded toward hers. "You need to put that under cold water. And it would help to cover it with sterile gauze. Cutting off the air will ease the discomfort and protect the skin. I have some if you need it."

"Thanks. I'll be fine."

She worked her feet into her flip-flops, then retrieved her mug and book and shoved them into the beach bag—all the while keeping tabs on him. Slinging the canvas tote over her shoulder, she folded up her chair, tucked it under her arm and started toward the stairs.

The thought of her trying to navigate the steep, narrow steps in her condition while juggling the chair and tote sent a chill down Luke's spine.

"Why don't you let me help you with some of that?" He fell in behind her.

Throwing an alarmed glance over her shoulder, she picked up her pace. "I can manage. I do this all the time. Thanks." The expression of gratitude was tacked on, like an afterthought.

He fell back, watching as she plunged into the tall grass and followed the faint path, holding his breath while she labored up the wooden steps. When she took a quick look back toward the beach from the top, he raised a hand in farewell.

She ignored him.

Five seconds later she disappeared, heading toward the small bungalow tucked among the trees that he'd noticed from his bedroom window this morning.

Talk about strange encounters.

Shaking his head, he picked up his mug and moved farther down the beach, near the edge of the property line. As far away from the pregnant blonde's spot as possible. They might have to share the beach, but it was big enough for both of them. Better yet, his privacy should be safe. His neighbor didn't strike him as the warm, friendly, talkative type.

As he unfolded his chair, Luke tried to look on the bright side. If he had to have a neighbor, at least she wasn't part of some large, noisy family with a passel of kids who would disrupt his coveted and much-anticipated beach time.

Of course, it was possible his aloof beach mate had a husband or boyfriend or kids stashed in the bungalow. But some sixth sense told him she was here alone.

So where was the baby's father? Why wasn't he here to help her carry stuff up and down the steps?

Not your problem, Turner.

Determined to put his solitary neighbor out of his mind and enjoy the expansive view of the sparkling lake, Luke settled into his chair. He'd spent the past ten years caring about people in distress. Sometimes too much. Combat medicine was brutal, the injuries grievous, the mortality rate high. Eventually, the loss of life ate at your gut. He was here to heal. To keep a promise. To move on.

The last thing he needed was one more person to worry about.

As she held her hand under the cold running water in her kitchen sink, Kelsey Anderson focused on the dazzling expanse of blue water stretching to the horizon.

In the four months since she'd moved into the sturdy little cottage that had been built to withstand the brutal winter winds and ice of the Michigan lakeshore, this view had always calmed her. It carried her back to the carefree visits of her youth, when she and her parents and sister had come here for two or three weeks every summer. And it was the same view that had consoled her when she and Gram came alone all the summers after her mom died, while her dad had been working and her older sister had been busy with her part-time job.

But thanks to a tall, dark-haired man with broad shoulders, a powerful chest and biceps that were more scary than impressive, it didn't console her today.

If she had to have a neighbor, why couldn't it have been a single woman? Or an older couple? Or a family?

Why did it have to be a strong, lone male?

A shiver ran through her, and she turned off the tap. But memories, not cold water, accounted for her sudden chill. Memories she'd been trying hard to contain. And she'd done a good job of that.

Until today.

Taking a calming breath, she examined the coffee burn on the back of her right hand. A blister had formed, and when she flexed her fingers the patch stung. Her neighbor had suggested she cover it with gauze, but how many people kept gauze in their house? A Band-Aid would have to suffice.

As she rummaged through her first aid supplies in the bathroom vanity, she tried not to let the stranger's appearance ruin her day. But she always looked forward to her solitary Saturday mornings on the beach. She relished those quiet early hours before she opened her quilt shop for the weekend.

That peaceful interlude wasn't going to happen today, though.

And perhaps not again until her neighbor left.

Unfortunately, he'd mentioned being here for a few weeks. That would take them to the end of summer—and the end of morning weather conducive to sitting on the beach.

But maybe the allure of the sand and surf would wear off for him after a few days, and she'd have it to herself again. That often happened with visitors.

At least she could hope.

* * *

The view was great, and Luke shifted around in his beach chair, trying to unwind and enjoy it. But he couldn't find a comfortable position. Instead of chilling out, he felt restless—and more than a little guilty. He was sorry now about chasing off the jittery blonde. She seemed as much in need of a quiet respite as he did.

His relaxing morning a bust, Luke gave up. He had things to do anyway. Unpack, stock up on some groceries in Douglas or Saugatuck, get his thoughts together for Monday's meeting. He could try the beach again tonight. Watch the sunset, perhaps. They were supposed to be spectacular around here.

After draining his mug in the sand, he rose, he folded up his chair and set off for the steps.

As he waded through the tall grass, a book lying in the sand caught his eye. The one the blonde had shoved into the top of her beach bag before her hasty departure.

He bent to retrieve it, flipping the cover over to read the title: *Banishing Fear—How to Find Courage in Christ.*

A woman of faith. Interesting.

An interesting title, too.

What was his neighbor afraid of? And why was she seeking courage?

Weighing the book in his hand, he debated what to do with it. He doubted she'd appreciate him showing up at her door. Especially holding a book with a revealing title like this. But he couldn't leave it in the sand, either.

She had a back porch, though. He'd glimpsed it this morning from his bedroom window. If he left it there, there'd be no need for face-to-face contact.

Decision made, he started up the steps. It was a long haul, and despite his stringent exercise regime, he was breathing harder after the steep climb. As he paused at the top, he glanced at the back of the bungalow next door, visible through the trees that divided the properties. The trek up would have been a lot tougher for his pregnant neighbor. Based on the quick glimpse he'd gotten when her towel had slipped, she was seven or eight months along—and she'd been lugging a lot more stuff than he was.

Yet she'd refused his offer of assistance.

A woman of mystery, no question about it.

He made a quick detour to lean his beach chair against one of the two Adirondack chairs behind Mark's Cape Cod-style, white clapboard house, setting his mug on the chair's broad arm. Then he crossed the lawn, circled around the woods and headed for his neighbor's porch.

His step faltered, however, as the screened structure came into view.

She was inside.

He'd have turned around at once—except he didn't like what he saw. She was balanced on a ladder, reaching toward the fixture in the ceiling. Attempting to change a lightbulb.

And the ladder didn't look any too stable.

He lengthened his stride.

All at once, as if to reinforce his conclusion, the ladder wobbled. As he broke into a sprint, she clutched at the sides, dropping the replacement bulb in the process. He heard it shatter as he took the two porch steps in one leap, opened the door and grabbed for the ladder, tossing the book he was carrying onto a wicker settee.

His sudden appearance seemed to rattle her as much as the wobbling ladder had. Sucking in a sharp breath, she tried to descend quickly. But she missed a rung, and Luke relinquished his grip on the ladder to catch her when she slipped backward.

As his arms went around her and he absorbed her weight, he heard her panicked gasp. Felt the tremors coursing through her. Sensed her almost palpable fear.

And when her oversized T-shirt slipped off one shoulder, he also saw the jagged scar of recent vintage near her collarbone.

"You're okay." He gentled his voice, his focus still on the scar. "I've got you. Take a few deep breaths."

If she heard him, she gave no indication. Instead, she jerked out of his arms and stumbled toward her back door. As if she was running away.

Again.

As she fumbled with the knob, her back to him, he tried to reassure her.

"Look—I just came over to return your book. You must have dropped it on the beach."

She froze. Checked him out over her shoulder.

He tipped his head toward the book on the settee.

Flicking a look in that direction, she blushed. Then she turned halfway toward him, keeping one hand on the knob. As if prepared to flee at the slightest provocation. "Thank you."

"No problem." He gestured toward the ladder. "I think you need to replace that. It's seen better days."

"I will."

"In the meantime, why don't you let me change the bulb for you?"

"That's not necessary. Thank you."

Let it go, Luke. She doesn't want your help.

Even as that advice echoed in his mind, Luke found himself pushing—for reasons that eluded him.

"I don't mind. Might as well finish the job, as long as the ladder's out."

Without waiting for a reply, he repositioned the ladder and climbed up two rungs. Then he angled toward her expectantly.

She lifted her head and regarded him in silence, her expression uncertain.

He waited her out. Trying to maintain a pleasant, nonthreatening demeanor. Trying to figure out what was going on with his skittish neighbor. And trying not to get distracted by the wide green eyes fringed with thick, sweeping lashes, that had been hidden behind sunglasses earlier.

At last, she fumbled for the knob behind her. "Okay. Give me a minute."

With that, she disappeared inside. The door shut behind her. And though he was a few feet away, he heard the lock quietly slide into place.

Did he come across as that untrustworthy? Or was there some other reason for his neighbor's extreme caution?

Like that scar?

As he puzzled over those questions, he heard the lock again. A moment later, she exited, bulb in hand. Moving toward him, she stayed as far back as possible and held it up.

He had to lean sideways to reach it. As soon as the transfer was made, she retreated to the door.

After unscrewing the old bulb, he inserted the new one and rejoined her on the porch floor. He spoke over his shoulder as he folded up the rickety ladder.

"Where would you like this?"

"Just set it against the wall for now."

He did as she asked. He wasn't crazy about her carrying the heavy old wooden ladder, but it was better than her climbing on it. And he suspected he'd pushed enough for one day.

Brushing off his hands, he moved to the porch door—trying to give her the wide perimeter of personal space she seemed to require.

"By the way, I've staked out a spot at the far end of the beach. That way, we'll each have our privacy."

"Okay."

"Well…see you around."

She didn't respond. But as Luke descended the steps and crossed her lawn, he had the feeling she was watching him leave.

And hoping she *wouldn't* be seeing him around.

He was back.

Kelsey couldn't see him in the darkness. But she knew he was there. She could feel his presence. Behind her. Or in the woods on either side of her. Somewhere close.

Too close.

She had to get away.

Increasing her speed from a jog to a run, she pushed herself forward. Beads of sweat formed on her brow and began to trickle down her face. She shouldn't have come out here alone at night.

Panic surged through her, and she ran harder. Trying to elude her pursuer.

But she couldn't. He was faster. Stronger. She could hear his ragged breathing as he drew closer.

A sob rose in her throat. There were lights up ahead. People. Activity. In another two minutes she'd—

A hand gripped her arm.

Another clamped over her mouth.

She was yanked backward and dragged into the woods. She kicked. Twisted. Scratched. Nothing loosened the man's vise-like grip. He slammed her to the ground. Pressed a knife to her throat. Told her if she screamed she'd die.

Waves of terror washed over her, sucking her down, down, down. And then the screams came anyway. Over and over and…

Kelsey shot upright in bed, chest heaving as she gasped for breath and choked back the terrified cries clawing their way past her throat. Slowly, the familiar outlines of her cozy room came into focus, illuminated by the soft light from the lamp she lit each night to keep darkness at bay.

She was safe.

Choking back a sob, she closed her eyes and forced herself to take deep, even breaths. To focus on a mental picture of the placid, sparkling lake outside her bungalow. To imagine drinking the rich hot chocolate Gram used to make.

The comforting images worked their magic. Her heart resumed its normal rhythm. Her respiration slowed. Her shaking subsided.

When she felt steadier, she swung her feet to the floor and stood, one hand resting on the new life growing within her as she padded through the snug bungalow, double-checking every lock. It had been more than three months since she'd had such a graphic dream. Once she moved here and settled into Gram's house, they'd dissipated. Here, she'd felt safe.

But things had changed. Thanks to her new neighbor.

And he was going to be around until the end of the summer.

With a sigh, Kelsey made her way back to her bedroom.

It was going to be a long few weeks.

Chapter Two

"Teatime, my dear."

Setting aside the pattern she'd been sketching, Kelsey swiveled away from her desk and toward the front of Not Your Grandmother's Quilts. Dorothy Martin stood a few feet away, holding a delicate china cup of tea—and a plate containing two mini homemade scones.

Kelsey shook her head and smiled as she took the offering. "If you keep spoiling me like this, I'm going to have twenty extra pounds to lose after I have this baby."

The older woman waved her objections aside and tucked one stray strand of white hair back into her perfect chignon. "Nonsense. You haven't gained enough weight, if you ask me."

"The doctor says I'm fine."

"Hmph." Dorothy fingered the single strand of pearls around her neck, skepticism quirking her mouth. "You look tired to me. And you seemed a little stressed on Saturday. I meant to get over here and visit with you, but we were swamped."

"Maybe I shouldn't have talked you into letting me rent half your space for my shop. You've had to turn customers away at Tea for Two ever since I moved in."

"Don't be silly. It was a fine idea. This place was way too big for me." She dropped her voice to a conspiratorial whisper and leaned closer. "I'm seventy-five years old, Kelsey, even if I don't look a day over sixty-five." With a wink, she straightened. "I'd have retired if you hadn't made me that offer. This lets me keep my finger in the business without as much pressure. Serving a light lunch to fifty is a lot easier than dealing with two or three times that many people. This has worked out well for both of us."

"I know *I've* benefited. I get perks like this." She lifted her cup. "I'm not sure what you get out of the deal."

"Companionship." The older woman's usual sunny expression dimmed a few watts. "I surely do miss your grandmother. She used to drive into Douglas for a visit almost every afternoon. I looked forward to our chats—even if she did insist I serve her tea in a mug." An affectionate smile tugged at the older woman's lips.

In the silence that followed, Kelsey took a sip of the herbal tea from her china cup. How Dorothy and her grandmother had ever connected was beyond her. They'd been as different as two women could be. Dorothy wore silk, cherished tradition and liked order. Bess Anderson had favored jeans, loved to experiment with new ideas and thrived in chaos.

But they'd shared common values, lively intellects and kind hearts. Apparently that had been enough to seal their friendship for more than forty years.

"Gram was one of a kind, wasn't she?" The words came out choked, and Kelsey set the cup back on the saucer.

"That she was." Dorothy patted her arm, then straightened her own shoulders. "And she wouldn't want us to be moping around on her behalf. I never did meet a person who could wring more joy out of a day than Bess Anderson. I expect she'd be disappointed if we didn't follow her example."

"I agree. It's just harder some days than others to do that."

Dorothy gave her a keen look. "Any particular reason why it's harder today?"

Kelsey lifted one shoulder. "I haven't slept very well the past two nights."

The older woman wrinkled her brow. "Bad dreams again?"

"Yes." Dorothy was one of the few people who knew Kelsey's story. Her grandmother's nevermarried best friend had always been like a cherished great-aunt, and since Kelsey had moved to Michigan, Dorothy had done her best to fill the role vacated by Gram.

"How odd. You've been doing so well. Did something trigger them?"

"Not some*thing*. Some*one*. My new neighbor. A man in his thirties who's staying at the Lewis house. Alone, as far as I can tell." She traced the delicate gold-edged rim of the saucer with a fingertip. "He came up behind me on the beach Saturday."

"Oh, my." Distress tightened Dorothy's features. "I can see how that would have been upsetting."

"To make matters worse, I dropped a book while I was down there, and when he came by to return it I was changing a lightbulb on the porch. I was so startled I fell into his arms. Literally. I almost hyperventilated."

The bell over the front door jingled, announcing the arrival of tearoom customers, and Dorothy called out to the two women who entered. "I'll be right with you." Then she leaned closer to Kelsey and lowered her voice. "Maybe you should talk to Dr. Walters again."

"Maybe." She'd made weekly trips to the therapist in Holland during her first six weeks in Michigan, but her visits had tapered off as the nightmares grew less and less frequent. She hadn't been to see the woman in more than two months.

Now the nightmares were back. Thanks to Luke Turner.

As Dorothy seated her luncheon guests on the other side of the building, Kelsey forced herself to focus on more pleasant thoughts. Nibbling at a blueberry scone, she examined the row of quilts, displayed on large racks, that separated Tea for Two from Not Your Grandmother's Quilts in the high-ceilinged space they shared. The two in the middle were Gram's, and they were stunning. Creative, contemporary and abstract, they were pieces of art—and not at all what most people pictured when they heard the word quilt.

The ones on either end were hers. One was a commissioned piece she'd finished a couple of weeks ago and would soon be shipping off to the buyer. The other—an intricate, modernistic, three-dimensional design—wasn't for sale. Gram had praised it highly, calling it a breakout piece when Kelsey had sent her a photo of it last year. It had taken her three years to make, squeezing in a few minutes of work on it here and there. As she'd discovered, climbing the corporate ladder left little time or energy for anything else, including artistic pursuits. In fact, after finishing that piece she'd considered setting aside her beloved pastime for the indefinite future.

Yet now she was making quilts full-time.

It was surreal.

The baby kicked, and Kelsey placed a hand on her stomach—awed by the flutter of new life within her, even as it evoked traumatic memories.

It was a dichotomy she had yet to reconcile.

Her phone rang, and she swiveled back to her desk to answer it. As she picked up the receiver and prepared to switch gears, the baby kicked again.

Reminding her that the momentous decision she'd been struggling with couldn't be deferred much longer.

Luke pulled into a parking space in front of the St. Francis rectory in Saugatuck, picked up his briefcase and stepped out of the car. The small adjacent church looked just as Carlos had described it—traditional in design, with elongated panels of stained glass on each side and a steeple that soared toward the blue sky.

This was where the medical corpsman had turned his life around.

This was where he'd hoped to return and make a difference in the lives of other young people.

This was where his funeral had been held two short months ago.

Luke swallowed past the lump in his throat, forcing back a surge of emotion. The time for tears was past. He was here to look to the future. To do his part to fulfill a young man's dream. To keep a promise.

With one more look at the soaring steeple, he strode toward the door of the rectory and pressed the bell.

Thirty seconds later, a middle-aged man dressed in black and wearing a clerical collar answered. His smile created a fan of wrinkles at the corner of each eye as he stuck out his hand.

"Captain Turner, I presume. Or do you prefer Doctor?"

"Luke is fine. Father Reynolds?"

"Make it Father Joe. Come in, come in. I've been looking forward to your visit. Everyone is here, eagerly waiting to meet you." He closed the door and led the way down the hall. "May I offer you a beverage?"

"Coffee would be good, if you have it."

"Always." The man grinned and veered to his left at a T in the hall, leading Luke into a small, homey kitchen. He headed straight for the coffeepot on the counter, pulled a mug off a hook and filled it. "There's a carafe of coffee and disposable cups in the conference room, but the guest of honor deserves the real thing." He lifted the ceramic mug. "Do you take cream or sugar?"

"I like it black."

"So do I." The clergyman handed him the coffee and retraced his steps, continuing past the T. "We rotate our meetings among participating churches, and it happened to be my turn. Appropriate, since this was Carlos's church."

A few seconds later, the man ushered him into a small conference room dominated by a large rectangular table. Six people of various ages sat around it. As he entered, their conversation ceased and they all looked toward him.

"My fellow clerics, our guest of honor has arrived."

As Father Joe went through the introductions and Luke shook hands with each of the board members, he did his best to file away their names.

Once the formalities were finished, Father Joe gestured Luke toward the seat at the end of the table, then took his place at the other end.

"First, on behalf of the Greater Saugatuck Interdenominational Youth Fellowship, I want to thank you for initiating this project and for making such a personal investment in it. Your willingness to devote a significant amount of time to the planning and organizing has impressed all of us." Father Joe beamed at him.

Heat rose on Luke's neck, and he shifted in his seat. "I appreciate your kind words, Father, but my sacrifice is small in comparison to Carlos's. I'm giving time. He gave his life."

"Yes. Saving others. 'No greater love…'" The priest grew somber and folded his hands on the table. "Before we begin, shall we join our hearts in prayer?"

As they bowed their heads, the pastor spoke. "Father, we thank You for giving us the opportunity to gather here as Your family. Like all families, we are diverse. And we don't always agree. But You have opened our hearts and minds to allow us to seek our commonalities, and to unify behind the shared goal of supporting our youth and helping them grow in faith.

"We live in a difficult world, Lord, one where

young people can easily be led astray. Here, in our program, they can find acceptance and love and guidance. We ask that You give us fortitude and inspiration as we go about Your work. We thank You for letting our lives be touched by an inspiring young man like Carlos Fernandez. And we thank You for sending Captain Taylor to us with a plan that will honor him by helping us carry on the work that changed his life."

After a chorus of "amens," Father Joe turned the meeting over to Luke, who pulled his notes from his briefcase and gave the board an outline of the project he and Father Joe had corresponded about over the past few weeks.

Although Carlos's pastor had assured Luke the board was receptive to his idea, the enthusiastic response of the members was heartening.

But also a little unsettling.

Because, while Luke had come here to get the ball rolling for a youth center, the more the board members talked, the more it sounded as if they expected him to deliver said center in the short six weeks he would be in the area.

Catching his eye during an animated discussion about one fundraising idea, Father Joe smiled.

"Gentlemen—I think we're overwhelming our benefactor. Why don't we let him tell us what he would like to accomplish during his stay here, and see what we can do to assist him?"

Seven sets of eyes focused on him and the room grew quiet.

Luke cleared his throat and folded his hands on the table. "I'd be thrilled if we could break ground for this center before I leave. But realistically, that event may be a year or two down the road. If I learned one thing in the military, it was that nothing happens fast when a committee is involved."

A knowing chuckle rippled around the table.

Luke flashed them a smile. "What I hoped to do during my stay was work with you to set everything in motion. That would include developing a fundraising plan, spreading the word about the project and helping line up appropriate resources and benefactors to support the project long-term. I'm not an expert at this sort of thing, but I'm hoping we can draft the assistance of some local people who are."

"I agree we need to pull in experts." A thin, middle-aged man with a receding hairline spoke. Reverend Matthew Howard, Luke recalled. "None of us have the time or expertise to make this center happen. But there are plenty of experts in our own community who could take on pieces of this. One in my own congregation, in fact. She's a relative newcomer to the area. Kelsey Anderson. She runs a quilt shop in Douglas, but until earlier this year she was the director of public relations and corporate promotions for a large firm in St. Louis."

When the man named the well-known company,

Luke's eyebrows rose. "That's impressive. She sounds like just the kind of person we need."

"I agree." Father Joe leaned forward. "I haven't met Ms. Anderson, but I've heard about her. One of the women in my congregation mentioned taking some classes at her shop. Would you like to approach her, Matt?"

"I'll be happy to lay the groundwork. But I think the appeal would be more effective coming from Captain Turner." The man opened a file and removed a letter. A copy of the first one he'd sent to Father Joe, Luke noted. "Father Joe shared your initial query letter with all of us. It was quite moving. No one would be able to speak as passionately—or convincingly—as you about how your friendship with Carlos motivated you to take this on. If I set up a meeting with Kelsey, would you be willing to pitch your idea and solicit her involvement?"

"That's just the kind of thing I was hoping to do while I'm here." Luke encompassed the group as he spoke. "If any of you want me to meet with possible supporters, I'm happy to do so. And Ms. Anderson sounds like the perfect person to talk with first."

By the time the meeting broke up half an hour later, the board had compiled a list of resources, from the owner of the piece of property they hoped would someday be the site of the youth center, to the mayor of Saugatuck, to the manager of the hotel where Carlos had worked during his high school years.

As Father Joe led him out after all the others had left, the pastor paused in the small foyer, a twinkle in his eye. "I hope you weren't planning too much R & R during your visit to Michigan. With the to-do list we've already compiled, you won't have a lot of downtime. We clerics are great delegators, you know."

The whisper of a smile tugged at Luke's lips. "That's okay. I didn't come here to play."

"Good thing." The man studied him, his hand on the knob. "Not many people would take on a selfless job like this, Luke. I know you and Carlos worked together, and I understand that strong friendships can be forged on the battlefield. But I can't help thinking there's more driving you to take on this project."

Doing his best to keep his features neutral, Luke clenched his fingers around the handle of his brief-case. "I saw a lot of death overseas, Father. A lot of wasted potential. A lot of soldiers whose dreams died when they did. I can't change that. But it is within my power to make one man's dream come true. It seemed like a fitting way to end my military career."

"Ah. Closure." The older man nodded. "Well, you picked a worthy dream to pursue. And a fine young man to honor."

"The best." Luke's voice hoarsened, and he cleared his throat.

Father Joe opened the door and scanned the blue sky, giving Luke a chance to regain his composure. "What a beautiful day. Why don't you take advantage of it before Matthew calls and sends you off to see Kelsey Anderson?"

"I think I'll do that." Luke stepped past him, then turned to shake his hand. "Thank you for coordinating this."

"The thanks are all ours." The man clasped Luke's hand within both of his. "God go with you, Luke."

"I'm counting on it."

"You may. He never fails those who put their trust in Him."

As Luke strode toward his rental car, he raised his eyes to the heavens above the church, tracing the outline of the cross that soared toward the sky. God *had* gone with him so far. While many of his comrades had lost their faith amid the carnage of war, his had held fast for years. But finally, bone-weary from the constant onslaught of senseless death and man's inhumanity to man, his faith had faltered, too.

In the end, though, God had sent Carlos into his life. A young man whose heart burned with love for the Lord. Who had reminded him that in the midst of trauma and tragedy, good survived. Hope endured. Dreams flourished. Working with him day after day, watching him give tirelessly with a compassion that put the Good Samaritan to shame, had reinvigorated Luke's own faith.

Even as he lay dying, the young medic had been a source of inspiration. His eyes had been filled with the kind of peace that only comes from knowing you've done your best to follow the precepts of the Lord and are ready to meet Him face-to-face. His one regret, he'd told Luke, was that his dream to help young people back home would never be realized.

As he'd held the young man's hand, watching his life slip away while artillery shells burst around them, Luke had choked out a promise that his dream wouldn't die.

Gratitude had smoothed the lines of pain from Carlos's face, and he'd summoned up the last of his strength to speak. When Luke leaned close, he'd whispered, "Thank you."

And then the medic had tightened his grip and uttered two short sentences Luke would never forget.

"Let not your heart be troubled, my friend. God will bring good from this."

Moments later, Carlos's hand had grown slack in his.

The outline of the soaring cross blurred, and Luke blinked to clear his vision. His faith wasn't as strong as Carlos's. Especially after ten brutal years of treating battlefield injuries. But he intended to make certain at least one good thing came from the young man's death.

And as he unlocked his car and slid behind the wheel, he renewed the vow he'd made that day in

Afghanistan. Before he left Michigan in six weeks, the youth center Carlos had dreamed of would be well on its way to becoming a reality.

Whatever it took.

Chapter Three

The bell over the front door of the shop jingled behind her, and Kelsey checked her watch as she typed the final figures into the spreadsheet on the computer. Ten o'clock. On the dot. It had to be the army doctor her pastor had called about yesterday. He'd said the man would stop by around ten. And the military was nothing if not regimented.

"Give me one sec." She threw the comment over her shoulder as she hit Save. She wasn't thrilled about dusting off her PR skills or opening the door to her old life, but it was hard to say no to a godly man like Reverend Howard. And the youth center project did sound worthwhile. Besides, it wouldn't kill her to consult with the doctor for an hour, considering the amount of time *he* was investing.

Summoning up a smile, she swung around in her chair. "I'm sorry to keep you wai—"

The breath whooshed out of her lungs.

Her new neighbor stood six feet away. The one with the broad shoulders and impressive biceps.

Not that his biceps were on display today. Instead of a chest-hugging T-shirt and shorts, he was wearing a sport coat with a subtle herringbone pattern, tan slacks and spit-and-polished dress shoes. He looked professional. Reputable. Honorable.

And as stunned as she was.

"Kelsey Anderson?"

She opened her mouth to respond.

Nothing came out.

No surprise there. It was hard enough to breathe, let alone speak, with the man towering over her. Making her feel small. Vulnerable. Powerless.

"Well…good morning! We don't often have gentlemen venture into our establishments."

At Dorothy's cheerful welcome, the man turned. Giving Kelsey a chance to catch her breath.

Thank You, Lord!

Her shop mate was still hidden from Kelsey's view by the man's tall form, but her words registered loud and clear. "Dorothy Martin. I own Tea for Two." A hand shot out to gesture toward the other side of the shop. "You must be the army captain Kelsey told me about. I was just making a tea and scones delivery to my lovely neighbor. She must be in the back. I'll be happy to get her…"

Kelsey gripped the arms of her chair and struggled to her feet. At the squeak of her chair, Dorothy peeked around the visitor.

"Oh. There you are, my dear. Did I interrupt a conversation?"

"No. I just arrived. And I'm afraid I startled Ms. Anderson." The army doctor moved toward her and extended his hand. "Luke Turner."

Kelsey inched closer, wiping her palm on her slacks before she placed her fingers in his. As their hands connected, he flicked a quick glance down.

"The burn seems to be healing well."

Dorothy tipped her head and set the tea and scones on the counter. "You two have met before?"

Kelsey tugged her hand free and took a step back. "Yes. Captain—Doctor—Turner is the new neighbor I mentioned to you." She tried to keep her inflection neutral, but Dorothy's sharp look told her the other woman had picked up her nervousness.

The slight narrowing of Luke Turner's eyes told her he had, too.

"My goodness!" Dorothy's hand fluttered to her chest. "What an odd coincidence!" She motioned toward the snack she'd delivered and raised an eyebrow at Kelsey. "If you'd like to talk in the tearoom, I could bring a pot out for you to share."

Kelsey thanked her with her eyes. The closer she was to her dear friend, the safer she'd feel.

"That would be lovely. Thank you, Dorothy." She inclined her head toward the other half of the shop and addressed Luke. "It will be more comfortable to have our discussion over there."

As she grabbed a pen and notebook off her desk, he surveyed the sturdy chairs around the table in the corner where she held classes. In truth, they would better suit his tall frame. He'd be more comfortable *here*. But much to her relief, he followed her to the other side without comment.

"You two go right ahead with your business while I put on a pot of tea." Dorothy deposited Kelsey's scones and china cup on a table for two, brushed a miniscule speck off the pristine white cloth, and hurried toward the kitchen.

Pulling out one of the dainty chairs, Luke held it while Kelsey sat. Then he took the one on the opposite side of the table. The furniture seemed undersized to his large frame, and Kelsey felt foolish for insisting they move their discussion to this side of the shop.

Best to dive in so he could be on his way as quickly as possible.

"Reverend Howard was very enthusiastic about your project when he called." She tried for a conversational tone, but her voice came out sounding stiff.

Luke regarded her across the snowy expanse of linen, the expression in his dark brown eyes unreadable. "Before we get to that, may I ask you a question?"

A caution bell rang in her mind. "About what?"

"About why I make you nervous."

She swallowed. "You don't make me nervous."

Arching his eyebrows, he inspected the plate in front of her.

She looked down. A pile of crumbs was all that was left of the scone she'd pulverized.

Warmth rose to her cheeks, and she clasped her hands in her lap. It was silly to deny the obvious. But neither was she about to explain her reaction to this stranger.

When the silence between them lengthened, Luke rested his elbows on the table, steepled his fingers and frowned. "Have we ever met before that day on the beach, Ms. Anderson?"

"No."

"Then I must have done something to offend—or alarm—you during our short acquaintance."

"No. You haven't." She took a deep breath. "This isn't a personal issue, Captain—Doctor—which do you prefer?"

"I prefer Luke." He pinned her with an intent gaze and let a few beats of silence tick by. "Let me be honest. This youth center is too important to fall victim to a personality…quirk—for want of a better term. We need someone with your skills to help us build public awareness, but if you don't think we can work together, tell me now and I'll ask the board to suggest someone else."

Taken aback by his candor, Kelsey lifted her cup with shaky fingers and took a sip of tea. "You don't mince words, do you?"

"There's no time for indecision on the battle-field, Ms. Anderson. Nor do I have time to waste during my stay here. There's a lot to be done in six weeks."

Kelsey heard the foundation of steel under what sounded like a very faint Southern drawl. Luke Turner, it seemed, was a cut-to-the-chase kind of man, with little patience for indecisiveness.

"It must be nice to always be so certain about decisions."

She hadn't meant to speak that thought. Especially in a tone that was both wistful and reproachful. And the man across from her seemed as surprised by it as she was.

"I'm not certain how to interpret that." A defensive note crept into his voice.

"Here you go. A nice pot of tea and some more scones." Dorothy pushed through the door from the kitchen and hurried over with a laden tray. Luke rose and took it from her while she transferred the items to the table. "Thank you, young man. Such nice manners. A true Southern gentleman. That is a Southern accent I detect, isn't it?"

He smiled at her. "You have a good ear. I've been gone a long time, but I was born and raised in Atlanta."

"A fine city. Well, you two go right ahead with your chat. I'll be busy in the kitchen until my guests start arriving at eleven, but you just call out if you need anything and I'll be back in a jiffy."

The latter remark was directed to Kelsey, and she sent the older woman a quick smile of thanks.

When the door swung shut behind Dorothy, Kelsey turned her attention to the army doctor. Picking up the teapot, she filled his cup. "For the record, I never let personal feelings get in the way of a job. Now, in the interest of not wasting your time, why don't you tell me a little about the project so I can see if it's a good fit with my skills? Reverend Howard didn't give me many details. All he said was that you became friends with a medical corpsman from this area, and after he was killed you decided to spearhead an effort to build a youth center here in his honor, as part of the Interdenominational Youth Fellowship program."

"That about sums it up."

Kelsey set the teapot back on the table. Her pastor had also told her Luke Turner was passionate about the project. But she was picking up more caution than passion.

Her fault, no doubt. She'd treated him with nothing but suspicion and animosity in their few encounters. Yet from everything she'd heard and seen, he appeared to be a principled, compassionate…safe man. What could she have to fear from a former army doctor who was backed by a board of clergymen?

She forced herself to meet his eyes. "Captain Turner, I—"

"Luke."

"Luke." She moistened her lips. "The truth is, I'm a bit battle-scarred myself. And overly wary. I apologize if I've offended you. Maybe we should start over."

He gave a slow nod and lifted his cup. "I'll drink to that."

Following his lead, she picked up her cup, clinked it with his and took a sip. He did, too—then grimaced.

A smile tugged at her lips. "Not a tea drinker?"

One side of his mouth hitched up and he checked over his shoulder. "I don't want to offend Ms. Martin, but no. I like coffee. Strong and black. Just like Carlos did." His lips flattened.

"Would you mind telling me a little about him?"

At her quiet request, Luke stared into his tea. "We worked together for six months during my last deployment. I dealt with a lot of medics through the years, but Carlos was special. He was only twenty-two, but he had an amazing bedside manner. With just a look or a touch, he could instill trust and calm even in the most restless patient. After he got out, he wanted to be a paramedic. He would have been a good one."

His Adam's apple bobbed, and he took another sip of the tea he didn't want.

"Carlos grew up in Saugatuck. His mother was unmarried, and she went to her grave without revealing the name of his father. Carlos was only five when she died, and his grandmother took him in. They were poor, and he resented that—among other things. He got in with the wrong crowd in his freshman year of high school, and according to him, he gave his grandmother a lot of grief.

"But she was determined to straighten him out. So, after he was picked up on a minor shoplifting charge, she got together with the police chief and the shop owner, who were personal friends, and they worked out a deal. If he assisted Father Joe with the Interdenominational Youth Fellowship program for six months, the charges would be dropped."

"How did that go over with him?" Kelsey took a bite of her still-intact scone.

Luke's lips twitched. "Not well, according to Carlos. He agreed, but only under duress. However, much to his surprise, he liked the group—and the new pastor at his church. Father Joe became the father figure he never had. According to Carlos, Father Joe and the youth program turned his life around. Once he got out of the army and established his career, he wanted to start a fundraising drive to build a youth center for the program. A permanent place, where young people could gather instead of having to move from church hall to church hall."

"And when he died, you took that project on."

"Yes."

She studied him. "That's quite a commitment."

Luke dismissed her comment with a shrug. "I

needed some time to decompress from my deployment anyway. And this is a worthwhile project. It's a way to honor not just Carlos, but all the other young men and women who've given their lives in the line of duty. Whose dreams died with them. A lot of them passed through my hands. There were so many we couldn't save…." His words trailed off, and Kelsey saw a muscle twitch in his cheek.

The sudden pressure in her throat took Kelsey by surprise. She pushed her plate aside, folded her arms on the table and gave Luke a steady look. "Okay, you've convinced me it's a worthy project. And I'm comfortable we can work together." Not quite true, but she'd get past that. "Why don't you fill me in on the ideas you discussed at the board meeting yesterday, and I'll get back to you tomorrow with some initial thoughts."

He regarded her for a moment, his gaze measuring, and then a subtle warmth softened his eyes. "Fair enough."

For the next fifteen minutes, he gave her a rapid-fire summary as she scribbled notes. Her tea grew cold, but her heart warmed as the passion Reverend Howard had talked of intensified, convincing her Luke had, indeed, taken on Carlos's dream as if it were his own.

When he finished, she flexed her hand and smiled at the page she'd filled. "There's certainly plenty here to work with. I should have no trouble compiling some preliminary publicity ideas by tomorrow."

"Excellent." He smiled at her, and for some reason the tearoom suddenly felt too warm. "Now I've taken up enough of your time for one day." Setting his napkin on the table, he rose and extended his hand. "Thank you for meeting with me."

She stood, too. His fingers engulfed hers in a strong grip. "It's hard to say no to Reverend Howard."

"Father Joe's the same way." He released her hand. "We'll have to employ their persuasive skills in our fundraising efforts."

She grinned. "True. Few people do a better job of asking for money than the clergy."

Eyes glinting with amusement, he pulled a small notebook and pen from his jacket pocket, then bent down and jotted a number with bold strokes. A faint whiff of his appealing, rugged aftershave tickled her nose, and she found herself fighting a temptation to lean closer.

Thrown by the impulse, she gripped the back of her chair and held on tight.

He tore the small sheet of paper from the notebook and handed it to her. "That's my cell number. Why don't you call me when you're ready to continue our discussion?"

His lean fingers brushed hers, and her heart skipped a beat—then lurched into double time.

What in the world was going on?

"Kelsey?"

At his concerned query, she somehow managed to drag her lips into the semblance of a smile. "Yes. Good. I'll call you."

She tried not to squirm under his discerning perusal.

"Okay." He pocketed his notebook and pen. "I'll talk to you soon."

With that, he strode toward the front door and disappeared to the accompaniment of a cheery jingle.

Kelsey groped for the edge of the table and sank into the chair she'd vacated, trying to get her pulse under control.

This was not good.

For the past seven months she'd coped with mild panic attacks in the presence of powerful men. She was used to the shakiness. The feeling of being off balance. The adrenaline surge.

This time, however, her reaction hadn't been caused by fear, but by an equally unsettling emotion.

Attraction.

Kelsey closed her eyes and exhaled. No doubt Dr. Walters would call this progress and be pleased. But Kelsey wasn't. Because the man in question was here for a very short time on a mission that did not include romance.

Rising, she steadied herself on the edge of the table and ran a finger over the soft fabric that covered the scar on her shoulder. She couldn't let this flicker of attraction get out of hand. If she did, it could lead to heartbreak. And scars of a different kind.

And she'd already had enough trauma to last a lifetime.

Chapter Four

Luke paused at the top of the long flight of stairs that led to the lake, determined to finally watch a sunset from the beach. Based on the position of the yellow orb, he still had a good hour before it hit the horizon. And that was okay. He'd have plenty of time to eat the sandwich and chips he'd picked up in Saugatuck after his productive meeting with Dennis Lawson, the manager of the hotel where Carlos had worked during his high school years.

He drew in a lungful of fresh air, letting the stillness seep into his pores. Only after arriving in Pier Cove had he realized how parched his soul had been for peace and quiet—rare commodities in his prior life.

And they were his number-one priority for tonight.

Hoisting his beach chair to his shoulder, he started down the steep flight, juggling a cardboard tray containing a cup of coffee and a white deli bag in one hand while keeping a tight grip on the railing with the other.

Although his schedule today had been a cake-walk compared to the grueling pace and intensity of battlefield medicine, he was beat. Tension was so much a part of his life, it was difficult to relax. And that led to soul-deep weariness. The kind that sets in after too much stress over too much time. Today's meetings, which had all involved baring his soul a little beyond his comfort zone, hadn't helped, either. Dennis, as well as the mayor and the owner of the land the youth program hoped to buy, had all pressed for details about his experiences with Carlos.

His encounter with his neighbor this morning had also been taxing. In the beginning, anyway. At least they'd parted on better terms after their little tête-à-tête over tea. But she was the most inscrutable female he'd ever met.

Midway down, Luke paused on the landing to readjust his chair as he thought back over their conversation. He had no idea what several of her remarks had meant. Like the one about decisiveness. Had it been prompted by criticism or envy? And what had the comment about being battle-scarred meant? Was it related to the actual physical scar near her collarbone—or was she referring to emotional trauma?

With a shake of his head, he continued to the bottom, then pushed his way through the chest-high beach grass toward the open strip of sand. He was not going to let thoughts of his enigmatic neighbor ruin his evening. Whatever her problems, he had other things to—

His step faltered as he emerged from the grass.

The mystery woman was seated twenty feet away on the beach.

Wonderful.

Blowing out a frustrated breath, he sized up the situation. She'd chosen a spot a little to the right of the position she'd occupied on Saturday, angled away from the path. Like him, she was dressed in jeans. A loose fitting knit top disguised her pregnancy, and a jacket rested on the sand beside her, as did an insulated mug with a lid. She was hatless tonight, and the wind was ruffling her silky blond hair as she focused on a pad of paper in her lap.

In the distance, a family group was gathered around a bonfire. But she seemed as oblivious to their presence as she was to his.

Good. He hoped she stayed that way.

Skirting the beach grass, he worked his way down the sand in the other direction, until a good fifty feet separated them. While he opened his chair, sat and retrieved his sandwich from the white bag, he kept an eye on his neighbor. If he was lucky, she wouldn't notice him until she was ready to leave.

Unfortunately, his luck didn't hold that long. As he started on the second half of his turkey sandwich, she looked toward the horizon. A few seconds later, she turned her head in his direction.

And froze.

Luke stopped chewing and forced himself to raise a hand in greeting, as the manners his mother had instilled in him kicked in.

For a moment, he thought she was going to ignore him. Truth be told, he hoped she would. Then he could focus on the sunset in peace.

Instead, much to his surprise, she not only returned his wave, she called out to him. Although he strained to hear her words, the wind tossed them the other way, rendering them inaudible. Pointing to his ear, he shook his head.

She flipped her hand, as if to say forget it, and went back to her notepad.

Excellent. A reprieve.

He took another bite of his sandwich. Tried to focus on the horizon. But his gaze kept wandering back to his neighbor. There was something poignant and lonely about the solitary woman on the long stretch of windswept beach. The solitary *pregnant* woman. Poignant enough to prod him to his feet and push him toward her. His innate humanitarian instincts and sense of Christian charity gave him no option. Even if the selfish part of him said he deserved some time alone, he couldn't ignore her.

He called out as he approached, determined not to startle her this time. "The wind's blowing the wrong direction. I couldn't hear what you said a minute ago."

The setting sun cast a golden glow over her

complexion, gilding the ends of her long eyelashes and highlighting her model-quality cheekbones as she looked his way in surprise. The effect was so mesmerizing he had to force himself to pay attention to her words instead of her face.

"It wasn't important enough to interrupt your dinner." She gestured to the half sandwich in his hand.

He shrugged. "Not much to interrupt."

"I only said it was a beautiful evening. And that we should be in for a spectacular sunset."

He watched her lips as she spoke. They were nice lips. Full and soft and…

Luke cleared his throat. Shifted his attention to the horizon. Tried to focus on the clouds massing in the distance instead of on the image of her lips.

It didn't work.

How weird was that?

Fisting his free hand on his hip, he frowned at the view, trying to make sense of his reaction. He hardly knew Kelsey Anderson. Nor did his neighbor seem interested in changing that situation. Plus, the woman was pregnant. Maybe married. And she had baggage. Lots of it, he suspected.

There could be only one explanation for the unexpected tingle of attraction he'd just felt.

It had been way too long since he'd had a real date.

What else could it be?

He heard her stir behind him. No doubt wondering why he hadn't responded to her comment.

Say something, Turner.

"Yeah. I've been looking forward to my first sunset on the beach."

He pasted on a smile and forced himself to turn back to her—just as the capricious wind snatched a loose sheet of paper off her lap.

Luke took off after it, snagging it as it somersaulted down the beach. Sandwich still in one hand, he glanced at the neat, precise handwriting and the bullet-point outline Kelsey had been compiling.

A list of PR initiatives for the youth center project.

He scanned it as he retraced his steps. "Looks like you've been putting some serious thought into this."

She took the paper and slipped it into the middle of the tablet on her lap. "I promised you some suggestions tomorrow. I'm teaching a class in the morning, so tonight was my best chance to work on them. Besides, I get my most creative ideas here anyway."

He surveyed the landscape. "I can see why. And from the quick glimpse I got of your notes, it seems to have been a productive session. So what's your number-one recommendation?"

"Media interviews. If you're willing."

"Me?" His eyebrows rose.

"You have a great personal story to tell that will connect with potential donors and supporters."

"This is supposed to be about Carlos."

"It is." She leaned forward, her expression earnest. "And who better to tell the world about him than the man who worked alongside him on the battlefield? Who saw the transforming effect the youth fellowship had on his life. Who was so moved himself by Carlos's dream to help other young people benefit from that same program that he took on the task of turning the young medic's dream into reality, as a tribute to him."

He stared at her. With her defenses down, her green eyes flashing with enthusiasm and passion, Kelsey Anderson was stunning.

Wow.

The spark of attraction flared again, and Luke took a deep breath. Let it out.

Not part of the agenda, Turner.

"You're good." He strove for a businesslike tone. "If I wasn't already spearheading this campaign, I'd be ready to sign on the dotted line."

His praise brought a becoming flush to her cheeks, and she leaned back in her chair. "Creating buy-in and shaping public opinion was my job for a long time."

"And now you make quilts." *Why?* Luke didn't voice that question. But there was a story here. One he wanted to hear.

"And now I make quilts." She ignored his implied query, her unwavering gaze telling him to back off.

He did. For now. Afraid she'd retreat if he didn't.

"So what other ideas have you jotted down there?" Again, he gestured to the hidden sheet of paper.

She hesitated, then drew it out. "I'm not ready to talk about this in detail yet, but if you want to pull your chair over, I can give you a few highlights."

"Sold. I'll be right back."

As he retrieved his chair and the rest of his dinner, Luke didn't waste time analyzing his sudden change of heart about avoiding his neighbor. The reason was obvious. A pretty woman plus a guy who'd gone too long without a date added up to hormones. Nothing more. And there was no harm in enjoying the little flicker of attraction for a few minutes.

She took a sip out of her mug as he set up his chair beside her, and he tipped his head toward it. "More tea?"

"No. I get more than enough of the decaf and herbal versions at the shop. This is milk." She wrinkled her nose. "And I feel about it the way you feel about tea."

He didn't need to ask why she was drinking it.

"When is the baby due?" He lowered himself into his chair and stretched his legs out in front of him, crossing them at the ankles.

Her lips flattened, telling him two things. This

wasn't a subject she wanted to discuss. And her feelings about her pregnancy were mixed, at best.

A reaction that only raised more questions.

"September fifteenth." She gestured to the tablet. "We'd better talk about this before we lose the light."

Luke got the clue and did his best to switch gears. "Okay. I'm ready."

As she laid out her recommendations, he continued eating his sandwich.

In addition to media interviews, she'd come up with a dozen other ideas to garner public support and spread the word about the project, including a fundraising dinner, speaking engagements at local organizations, and a clever way to generate positive publicity for companies who donated goods to the cause, creating a win-win scenario.

When she finished, he shook his head. "All I can say is, you must have been very good at what you did in the corporate world."

Her cheeks pinkened as she slipped the sheet of paper back into the lined tablet and drained her mug. "It's not difficult to be successful when your job is your life. But that's not the healthiest way to live."

"Is that why you left? To get more balance?"

She bent down and settled the mug in the sand, hiding her face from his view. "Let's just say circumstances helped me realize I needed to realign my priorities. Spectacular sunset, isn't it?"

Luke checked out the sky. The sun had dipped to

he horizon, edging the clouds with gold and tinting he sky—and the beach—pink. It *was* spectacular. But he was more interested in the woman beside him.

"Yeah. Fabulous." Luke leaned back in his chair, out of her line of sight, and studied her. The setting sun continued to cast a warm glow on her profile. But it also highlighted the faint lines at the corners of her eyes that spoke of weariness and worry. Apparently, realigning her priorities hadn't erased either of those from her life. Why not? And what "circumstances" had made her ditch the fast track in the corporate world and move to her grandmother's cottage to make quilts? Where did the absent father of her baby fit into the picture?

The more he learned about Kelsey Anderson, the more intrigued he became.

Suddenly, as if sensing his scrutiny, she turned her head.

He transferred his attention to the sky at once. "I'm glad I didn't miss this."

"It beats anything on TV." With one more glance at the sky, she tucked her tablet under her arm and swung her legs to the side of the chair. "I'd stay to the end, but navigating those steps is tricky enough when the sun is shining. It's downright dangerous in the dark." Her voice sounded nervous, as if she'd once more wrapped herself in a cloak of caution.

As she struggled to extricate herself from the low-slung chair, Luke rose and held out a hand.

"You may need to switch to a regular lawn chair soon." He kept his tone light, hoping she'd accept his help. "They're a lot higher off the ground."

He waited while she considered his hand—and let out a sigh of relief when she took it. He didn't relinquish his hold until he was certain she was steady on the shifting sand.

"Thanks." She sounded a little breathless as she tugged her fingers free and reached down to fold up her chair and snag her jacket off the sand.

As it had the day of the lightbulb incident, her top slid off her shoulder, revealing the jagged scar near her collarbone. She tugged it back into position before he got a good look, but the quick glance she darted his way told him she was afraid he'd seen it. And was worried he might ask more questions.

He had plenty of those. But voicing them wouldn't be smart. If he wanted to know Kelsey's secrets, he'd have to give her time to get comfortable with him. To learn she could trust him.

Unfortunately, given her extreme wariness, that could take a whole lot longer than the six weeks he'd be in Michigan.

"I'll finish up my recommendation tonight and give you a clean copy tomorrow, if that's okay." She hoisted her chair onto her shoulder.

"Sure. Fine."

She started toward the path through the grass, and he fell into step beside her. "Why don't you le me carry that stuff up for you? It would be easy to trip in the dark, and that wouldn't do either of you any good."

Her step slowed as she eyed the steep flight of stairs ahead. "I've managed fine by myself so far."

"Things are only going to get tougher as you get bigger. As a doctor, I recommend you take whatever unsolicited help you can get. Unless you already have someone lined up to do the heavy stuff."

It was a backdoor way to confirm the baby's father wasn't around—and he doubted it would work.

But much to his surprise, it did.

"My sister will come if I decide—if I need help after the baby is born."

So the baby's father wasn't part of Kelsey's life. And wouldn't be in the future.

Was he the source of her scar? Had she been in an abusive relationship?

The notion didn't sit well with him.

"Okay. Thanks for the offer." Kelsey handed over her chair, interrupting his train of thought.

"Smart decision." He summoned up a grin. "I may be a doctor, but I don't want to have to treat a sprained ankle—or worse—while I'm here. Give me a sec."

He went back to retrieve his own chair, taking her arm as they traversed the uneven sand. At the narrow path through the grass, he let her precede him, following close behind her as she slowly made her way up the stairs.

"Believe it or not, I used to be…in great shape." She huffed out the comment as they reached the top.

Despite the dim light, he could tell her cheeks were flushed from the exertion.

"I expect you still are. Forty steps would make anyone breathe harder."

"They don't seem to have taxed *your* lungs."

"They would have if I'd been carrying an extra fifteen or twenty pounds." He tapped her chair, still slung over his shoulder. "Would you like me to take this over to your porch?"

"No. Thank you." She reached for it. "I can manage fine on flat ground. Good night." Gripping the chair in one hand, she crossed the lawn and disappeared through the trees that separated their property.

Luke stayed where he was until he saw the light in her kitchen flick on through the leafy branches. Then he turned toward the fading sunset. A few minutes ago, the sky had been a glorious palette of brilliant colors, the water alive with ethereal light. Now the heavens had faded to a dull, uninteresting gray, robbing the lake of its shimmering incandescence and leaving ominous, leaden shadows in its wake.

The change had been startling. And swift.

Though Luke had learned very little about Kelsey Anderson since their first encounter, he was beginning to sense the changes in her life had been equally startling. And swift.

But what had prompted them? And was her new life in isolated Pier Cove a permanent change? Or had she sought temporary refuge here to protect herself—and her unborn child?

Luke shook his head and lifted his free hand to massage his neck. He didn't want complications on this trip. The task he'd set himself was difficult enough. Worrying about his neighbor wasn't part of the plan. Nor would she welcome his concern if he expressed it.

Yet he wasn't the type to walk away from people in need. That was why he'd become a doctor. Why he'd done more than his share of gritty, heartbreaking work near the front lines. Why he'd promised a medic he'd create the young man's legacy in his stead.

But it was hard to help people who didn't want help. And maybe he wasn't supposed to help Kelsey. Maybe he was supposed to let this go.

Except he knew about loneliness. And disillusion. And anguish. He'd lived through all of them overseas. And Kelsey was living through them now. Every one of those emotions was reflected in the clear, green depths of her troubled eyes.

Tipping his head back, he looked toward the heavens, where stars were just beginning to peek out.

Lord, You led me here. For a mission I thought was clear. If You have another job in mind for me, would You let me know? Soon? And in the meantime, please let Kelsey feel Your healing presence. Because I have a feeling she's in desperate need of some divine guidance and a healthy dose of TLC.

Chapter Five

"Ah, Kelsey! What a nice surprise!"

At Reverend Howard's greeting, Kelsey looked up from her book and watched the middle-aged pastor cross the grass with his typical spry gait. Since he knew she often walked down to this small park in Douglas at lunchtime, his comment about being surprised seemed a bit odd.

Her curiosity piqued, she gestured to the facing seat in the double-sided swing she'd claimed on the edge of Kalamazoo Lake. "It's nice to see you, Reverend. Won't you join me?"

"Thank you. I will." He settled in across from her. "So what are you reading this fine day?"

She angled the book of baby names toward him.

He cocked an eyebrow. "Does that mean you've reached a decision?"

With a sigh, she rested her hand on her stomach and shook her head. "No. I'm just trying to be prepared for all contingencies."

"God will give you the answer in His time."

"The trouble is, I'm running *out* of time."

"You still have two months. And if you decide to give up the baby for adoption, all the arrangements are in place with the agency I contacted on your behalf. Try not to let the pressure get to you."

"It's hard not to, the way the weeks are flying by." She ran a finger down the spine of the book. "You know, a year ago, if someone had predicted that in twelve months I'd be pregnant, living in Gram's cottage and making quilts for a living, I'd have thought they were crazy. I was totally focused on my goal of being a vice president by the time I was forty." She shook her head. "So much for plans."

"Is your new life losing its luster?"

"Not at all. I don't miss the corporate rat race one iota. I may not make the big bucks anymore, but my life is more in balance and the creative work feeds my soul. I'm just sorry it took such a traumatic wake-up call for me to see the light." The baby kicked, and she touched her stomach. "I can even have a family if I want one."

"Raising a child alone is difficult, Kelsey. Especially under your circumstances."

At the minister's quiet comment, a pang echoed in her heart. They'd had similar discussions several times over the past few months, though he'd never before been as direct.

"Don't you think I'm up to it?"

"I think you are a very strong woman who can achieve whatever you set out to accomplish. Your success in the corporate world proves that. So does your decision to change your life in the face of opposition from family and coworkers. But this decision isn't just about you. It's also about what's best for your child. He or she deserves unconditional love, Kelsey."

"You don't think I can offer that?"

"Only you can answer that question. No one would blame you if you couldn't."

Tears pricked Kelsey's eyes, and she looked over the sparkling water, blinking them away. "I didn't think I could in the beginning. I wanted nothing to do with this baby. But now…" Her hand moved over her stomach. "I've felt him or her kick. I've seen the ultrasounds. I've heard the heartbeat. This child is part of me, Reverend. How can I give away part of myself?"

"I know it's a very, very difficult decision, Kelsey. One best made after much prayer. But whatever you decide, you've already done the noble thing by carrying the child to term. That's more than most people would expect."

Her jaw stiffened in resolution. "There was never a question in my mind about that."

"I admire the strength of your convictions. And you'll continue to be in my prayers as you wrestle with your decision." He leaned over and patted her hand. "Now I'll continue my constitutional, as my grandfather called it. A walk is good for body and soul, and a stroll through Douglas is always pleasant when business brings me here."

"I agree. Walking has become the centerpiece of my exercise program." Even after the baby was born, it would remain so. Kelsey had no further interest in jogging.

"Good, good." He slid out of the swing, but remained beside it, hands clasped behind him. "By the way, I spoke with Captain Turner this morning. He said you had a productive meeting yesterday. Two meetings, in fact."

Kelsey settled back in the swing. Now they were getting to the real reason for his noontime constitutional.

"Yes. He came by the shop. And then I ran into him on the beach near my cottage. Did he tell you we're neighbors?"

"He did. What a remarkable coincidence. But not a favorable one for you, he seems to think. I got the feeling he's concerned that his presence has been disruptive for you."

"It has been unsettling. As far back as I can remember, I've felt safe in Gram's cottage and on her beach. Pier Cove always seemed untouched by the world. Now, with a lone male so close by…" She let her voice trail off.

"Given your recent experience, I can understand how that would make you uneasy. But the captain strikes me as a man of honor and integrity. Someone to be trusted, not feared."

"I'm sure he is. Still, his presence…changes things."

"Some changes are good, as you've discovered in the past few months. Perhaps the captain's presence will be one of them." The minister leaned over and patted her hand again. "Give it a little time, my dear. As we've often discussed, God works in mysterious ways. And good can come of bad." With a wave of farewell, he headed back toward Center Street.

Kelsey watched him stride away. It was true that good had come of bad, though she would never have believed that on the cold December night in St. Louis when her life had changed forever. And in light of that, maybe Reverend Howard was right about Captain Turner, too. Maybe her new neighbor would turn out to be a blessing in disguise.

And that was an outcome definitely worthy of prayer.

Stomach growling, Luke slid a bowl of chili from Crane's Pie Pantry into the microwave and reached for one of the restaurant's famous cider doughnuts to stave off his hunger until his entree was ready. He should have stopped for lunch today, but after his trip to visit Carlos's still-fresh grave at Fort Custer National Cemetery, his appetite had vanished.

Now it was back with a vengeance.

As he devoured the doughnut, his cell phone

began to vibrate. At the familiar number on the digital display, he smiled and put the phone to his ear. "Hi, Mom."

"Oh, Luke, it's so good to hear your voice!"

Since his return from overseas, they'd talked almost every day, and she always greeted him with the same comment.

"You're going to get tired of hearing it once I move back to Atlanta and start mooching meals off of you."

"Never! I can't wait to make your favorite dinner the first night you're home."

His smile broadened. He could recite the menu by heart: Caesar salad, pork tenderloin, au gratin potatoes, green bean casserole and his mom's famous split lemon cake. It was the same menu she'd always prepared when he came home on leave. His salivary glands went into overdrive as he thought about it.

"That sounds a whole lot better than the chili I'm having tonight."

"Chili? That's all you're having for dinner?" Dismay raised the pitch of her voice.

"It's great chili. Or so I'm told. And I'm having homemade wheat bread and cider doughnuts, too. The doughnuts I can vouch for. They're fabulous." He licked a few grains of sugar off his finger.

"Not the healthiest menu I've ever heard. And not enough for a grown man. Now throw in some buttered grits…"

He grinned. Though Southern born and raised,

he'd never been a fan of grits. As his mother well knew. "I think I'll stick with the chili. Are you and Dad ready for your trip?"

"As a matter of fact, that's why I called."

The sudden hesitancy in her tone put him on alert. "Is everything okay? Dad isn't sick, is he?"

Luke would never forget the scare they'd all had three years ago, when his robust father's chest pains had led to bypass surgery. But he hadn't suffered a heart attack, and he'd been in good health since.

"My, no, he's fit as a fiddle. Out painting the tool shed in back as we speak. But we do have a little problem. You know how Hannah was supposed to stay with a friend for the three weeks we're in Europe? Well, that friend was in a car accident yesterday. She broke her leg and needs surgery, so we can't possibly impose on her family. They have enough on their plate."

He knew where this was heading, and the bottom dropped out of his stomach.

"Here's the thing, Luke," his mother continued. "I know you have a lot to do while you're up there, and I hate to infringe on your time, but is there any possibility you could take Hannah while we're gone? I wouldn't feel comfortable leaving her alone here by herself. Even though she's made it clear she's very capable of being on her own."

Luke raked his fingers through his hair. He had little spare time to entertain a seventeen-year-old. Besides, the age difference between him and his parents' late-in-life daughter had made them almost strangers.

Yet he knew his parents had been planning this grand tour of Europe for years, putting away a few dollars toward it from each of his father's modest paychecks. Paychecks that had mostly gone to feed, house and educate him and his sister. Buy birthday presents. Pay for braces.

Suck it in, Turner. Your parents deserve a worry-free trip. They made enough sacrifices for you.

"Sure, Mom. No problem. It will give Hannah and me a chance to get reacquainted."

"You're the best, Luke." A sniffle came over the line. "Course, I already knew that. Now, we're leaving on Sunday, but I surely would like this to all be settled and know she's safe and sound before the weekend. Would it be all right if we send her up on Friday?"

Day after tomorrow.

His stay in Michigan was getting more complicated by the day.

"That will work. I'm assuming she'll fly into Grand Rapids and I can pick her up there."

"That's what I'm hoping. As soon as I have the arrangements in place I'll call you back."

The microwave pinged, and his mother ended the call with a quick sign-off. "Enjoy your dinner and I'll talk to you soon."

Tapping the End button, Luke slid the phone back on his belt and pulled his chili out of the microwave.

But instead of taking it out to the backyard, as he'd planned, he slid it onto the kitchen table, cut a slice of homemade bread and pulled a tablet and pen out of one of the kitchen drawers. He needed to make a list of things to do before Hannah arrived.

As he dug into the chili, he wrote a few items down. Prepare one of the spare bedrooms. Make sure there were plenty of towels in the extra bathroom. Stock the kitchen with more than cereal and canned soup.

Then he ran out of steam. What kind of food did teenagers eat, anyway? For that matter, what did they do all day? Should he check out the local calendar of events? Find the location of the closest DVD rental place? Line up some activities for her? But what kind? What did she enjoy? He should have paid more attention to her periodic emails.

Overwhelmed, Luke set his spoon down and propped his chin in his palm.

What in the world was he going to do for three long weeks with a seventeen-year-old sister he hardly knew?

File folder in hand, Kelsey paused at the edge of the small copse of trees that separated her property from her neighbor's and peered at the Lewis house. Though it wasn't yet dark, a light was on in the kitchen. Meaning Luke was home. And with the sun already dipping low, it was unlikely he'd be heading down to the beach tonight to watch the sunset.

Too bad. She'd been keeping an eye on the steps from her window, hoping he *would* go down tonight. She'd planned to follow him, finished recommendations in hand, and pass them over down there. Somehow, that felt safer than doing it at the house where he lived. And ate. And slept. A beach seemed less personal. More public.

Safer.

Which was silly. A house was no different than a quiet beach or a screened porch or…a secluded jogging path.

Beads of sweat popped out on her upper lip, and she swiped them away in irritation. She had nothing to fear from Luke. Dorothy liked him. Her pastor spoke well of him. A board of clergymen endorsed him.

She could do this.

Squaring her shoulders, she marched over to his house. Stepped up to the deck and crossed to his door. Wiped her right palm on her jeans. Lifted her hand to knock.

Froze.

You are so pathetic, Anderson! Just rap your knuckles on that piece of wood and—

All at once, the door opened abruptly. With a gasp, she stumbled back.

Luke's hand shot out and gripped her arm. "Watch the steps behind—"

At his touch, she jerked free and scurried back, clutching the folder to her chest.

"Sorry." He stayed where he was and lifted his hands in a gesture of surrender. "Just be careful of the steps on the deck behind you."

Steps. Deck. Right. She'd come up a couple of them on her way to the door.

Angling toward the lake, she made a pretense of checking them out while she tried to quiet the thumping of her heart. When it refused to cooperate, she was forced to turn back anyway.

"Thanks. I forgot about them. I had this on my mind. My recommendations for your project." She held up the file, lamenting the tremor in her voice—and in the folder. Her hands were shaking. Warmth surged on her cheeks, and she clutched it with both hands, once more hugging it to her chest.

"I was just going to sit in one of the Adirondack chairs." He ignored her display of nerves, his tone casual. Calm. Soothing. Like he was talking to a frightened horse. "Would you like to join me and run over everything?"

She cast a wary look at the chairs. "Those seats weren't designed for mothers-to-be."

"Good point. Let's stay here, then." He gestured to a patio set on the deck. "Or we can use the kitchen table."

"Here is fine." No way was she entering the man's house.

Following her, he pulled out a chair, then took the one beside her as she withdrew a multipage document from the folder and handed it over.

He paged through it. "You've done a lot more work since we talked last night."

"Not really. I just fleshed out the ideas. Let me walk you through it."

For the next fifteen minutes, as she reviewed the document with him, Luke asked appropriate questions and made a few complimentary remarks. But he seemed distracted. As if he had other, more pressing, matters on his mind.

When she finished, Kelsey slipped the recommendations back into the folder and handed it over. "I'm used to dealing with the media and writing press releases, and I'll be happy to continue helping with those things. It's a worthwhile cause."

"I appreciate that." Luke tapped the folder against the top of the table, faint furrows creasing his brow.

Silence fell between them.

Kelsey shifted in her seat and scanned the vast expanse of blue water. Dark clouds were moving in and the wind was picking up, disturbing the placid surface. She should leave. A storm was approaching. Besides, the less contact with her disconcerting neighbor the better, right?

Right.

Then why was she hesitating?

One more quick peek at him gave her the answer. He, too, was focused on the horizon. And his face mirrored the turbulence in the lake.

"Luke…is everything okay?"

At her soft question, he blinked and shifted his attention to her. "Sorry. I'm a little distracted."

"I noticed."

One side of his mouth quirked up, but the worry in his eyes didn't dissipate. "My sister needs a place to stay for three weeks. She's arriving Friday."

"I take it her visit is unexpected?"

"Very."

He wasn't offering much, and Kelsey wasn't about to pry. Not after she'd rebuffed every attempt *he'd* made to ferret personal information from her.

Time to go.

She pushed her chair back and coaxed her lips into a smile. "Well, I won't take up any more of your evening. I'm sure you have a lot of things to do to get ready for your company."

"I'm sure I do, too." He blew out a breath. "I just don't know what they are."

Kelsey squinted at him. "What do you mean?"

He shook his head and raked his fingers through his hair. "Hannah is seventeen. She was in diapers when I left for college, and I haven't been home much since. We email some, but in my mind, she's still a freckle-faced kid with braces and pigtails and an overblown case of hero worship for her big brother. I have no idea how to entertain her for three weeks."

As he proceeded to explain the sequence of events that had led up to his mother's phone call, she pulled her chair back to the table and crossed her arms on the glass top.

When he reached the end of the story, she gave a sympathetic nod. "I can see why you feel obligated to do this. But the timing's not ideal, with the youth center project just starting up."

"Tell me about it. I'm not going to have a lot of time to spend with her."

"That might not be a problem. If she's like most seventeen-year-olds, she'll probably be happy to hang out on the beach, listen to music, watch DVDs and eat junk food."

"You think?" He gave her a hopeful look.

"Yeah, I do. But it's too bad she doesn't have someone her own age to hang out with. Maybe there's a youth fellowship activity or two that would appeal to her. You could ask Father Joe."

"Good idea."

A gust of wind whipped some strands of hair across her face, and Kelsey pushed them aside as thunder rumbled in the distance. Once more she slid her chair back.

"We'd better take cover. Lake storms can be nasty, and this one is approaching fast." As she spoke, she hoisted herself to her feet and examined the sky. The dark clouds had scuttled closer as they talked, erasing any evidence of the earlier blue sky. A raindrop plopped onto the glass-topped table, followed by another. "I'm out of here."

Grabbing the manila file folder, Luke followed

her to the edge of the deck. "Listen, I appreciate all your help with the project. And your encouragement. Hannah's a good kid. We'll work things out, I'm sure."

She stopped at the top of the steps and turned to him. "I am, too. But in case things go south for any reason, I was a seventeen-year-old girl once. A long time ago. I might be able to offer some advice."

"I'll take all the advice I can get. With Hannah, and with this." He waved the file folder as the rain intensified. "You better get home before you're soaked. Unless you want to sit out the storm in my kitchen over a cup of tea."

For a fleeting moment, she was tempted to accept his invitation. Odd, when half an hour ago she hadn't wanted to get anywhere near his house.

Before the temptation became too strong to resist, she shook her head and retreated down the steps. "Thanks, but this could be a long one. It might last all night."

There was a subtle shift in his eyes. Or perhaps it was just a shadow in the deepening twilight. Kelsey wasn't certain. And she didn't wait around to find out.

Calling a good-bye over her shoulder, she hurried toward her house.

By the time she reached her screened porch and slipped inside, the rain was coming down in earnest. Big drops pelted the ground, lightning slashed through the roiling black clouds and thunder boomed.

Kelsey moved into the safety of Gram's house, locked the door behind her and flipped on lights to dispel the gloom. Lake storms had never bothered her. They came in all blustery and ferocious, but when they were over, very little had changed. Pier Cove went on as before.

Too bad the storms of life didn't work the same way.

Yet if they had, she'd still be in the backbiting world of corporate politics. Still sacrificing any semblance of a personal life in pursuit of the gold ring of a vice-president slot. Still searching for happiness and fulfillment in the wrong place.

Still alone.

Pausing by the kitchen window, Kelsey rested her hand on her growing stomach and looked through the trees. Warm light spilled from Luke's windows, chasing away the stormy darkness.

Funny how a neighbor she hadn't wanted had so quickly worked his way into her life. All because of an idealistic, faith-filled young medic she would never know. Thanks to Carlos Fernandez, she'd met a man who was helping her heal. A man whose kindness, honor and unselfish generosity were starting to banish her fear. A man whose strength of character and steadfast principles were bolstering her trust and giving her hope for a future free of fear.

All of that was good.

But Luke Turner was doing one other thing, too. He was beginning to work his way into her heart as well as her life.

And considering his short tenure in Michigan, that could be bad.

Chapter Six

Was that Hannah?

Luke clutched a bouquet of flowers in one hand and a cup of Starbucks coffee in the other as he stared at the model-like young woman in the crowd of passengers emerging from the gate area of Gerald R. Ford International Airport in Grand Rapids.

He hadn't seen her in two years. She'd been away on a mission trip last year when he'd gone home on leave, and the year before he hadn't made it home at all. He took a closer look. Yeah, that was her all right. His mom regularly emailed family pictures, though they hadn't done his kid sister justice.

Nor had they prepared him for the fact that she wasn't a kid anymore.

Not by a long shot.

Spotting him, she smiled and waved. He didn't recognize the sleek, trendy hairstyle that feathered around her face and swept down her back, but he was relieved to see her eyes hadn't changed. She might have grown into a sophisticated young woman, but those baby blues hadn't lost their endearing sweetness and guileless charm.

Rather than head upstream of the crowd, he waited until she reached him.

"Hey, Luke." She stopped in front of him and gave him a wide, if slightly uncertain, smile.

He grinned and shook his head. "My little sister has morphed into a high-fashion model. When did you grow up?"

A pleased blush colored her cheeks. "According to Mom and Dad, I'm not there yet. That's why they foisted me on you. Sorry about that."

He waved the apology aside, enjoying her familiar drawl. "Nothing to be sorry about. This will give us a chance to catch up." He tossed his empty cup into a nearby trash container and pulled her to him. "How about a hug?"

Wrapping her in his arms, he held her close. The floral fragrance in her hair reminded him of the flowers in his hand, and when he released her, he held them out. "Welcome to Michigan."

She took them, burying her face in the assortment of roses, carnations and daisies. "This was really nice. Thank you, Luke."

"You're welcome." He made a mental note to pass the thank-you on to Kelsey. She'd suggested the flowers yesterday when she called to tell him about some radio interviews she was lining up. "Let's get your luggage and head home. Are you hungry?"

"Starved. All I had on the airplane was a tiny bag of pretzels."

"How does pizza sound? There's a good place in Saugatuck."

"That would be great."

As they waited for her luggage, she filled him in on her trip. Much to his relief, she wasn't resentful about the disruption in her summer plans with her friend, and she seemed to be genuinely looking forward to her beach time, assuring him she'd brought a bunch of paperbacks to read while she soaked up the sun.

By the time they were in his car and headed toward the lake house after dinner, the knot of tension that had formed between his shoulder blades after he'd agreed to host his sister began to unwind.

Hannah was a poised, self-sufficient young woman with her head on straight. Unlike many of her peers, she didn't have an attitude. She was easy to talk to, with a bubbly sense of humor that kept him laughing during much of the drive.

It seemed he'd been worrying over nothing.

This visit was going to be a piece of cake.

Yawning, Luke tucked his T-shirt into his shorts and padded barefoot into the kitchen. He'd slept far later than usual. But it was Saturday. And Hannah had assured him last night, after she'd settled in, that she didn't need a babysitter, that she was perfectly capable of getting her own breakfast and lunch, and that she might even try her hand at cooking a few dinners for them.

With his apprehensions eased, it was no wonder he'd passed out for ten solid hours.

A note on the dinette table caught his eye, and he strolled over to read it.

"At the beach. Couldn't wait to see it in daylight!" His sister had signed it in her scrawling hand.

Lips curving into a smile, Luke started a pot of coffee and filled a mug with milk for hot chocolate. Whenever he'd been home, that had always been Hannah's morning drink of choice. Maybe they could spend a relaxing hour or two on the beach together, catching up. And if Kelsey appeared, all the better. He suspected his neighbor and his sister would hit it off.

Things were definitely looking up on the home front.

While the coffee brewed, he shaved and grabbed a towel. Then he filled an insulated mug with the fresh brew and nuked Hannah's milk, stirring in a generous helping of chocolate. The second beach chair he'd placed on the deck was gone, so he grabbed the remaining one and headed down the steps.

As he waded through the beach grass at the bottom, he noticed two buff, twenty-something guys in swim trunks standing near the water to his right. Their backs were toward him, but they hadn't stopped to admire the view over the water. Instead, they were facing the small public beach only locals seemed to frequent, a short walk down the sand. They weren't looking at that, either, though. Their heads were bent.

Why?

The instant Luke cleared the beach grass, he had his answer.

Hannah.

Through their legs, he could see her reclining in her beach chair. Her head was tipped back, and she was smiling up at the college-age guys. He couldn't hear their banter, but he did hear masculine chuckles mingling with a flirty laugh that was way too adult to be coming from his baby sister.

His newfound peace of mind evaporated. No wonder his parents hadn't wanted to leave Hannah home alone.

Clearing his throat, he moved toward the small group.

The two college jocks angled toward him as he approached, and Hannah peeked around them, aiming a megawatt smile his way.

"Hi, Luke. Ah didn't wake ya'll, did I?"

One glance told Luke her two young admirers were eating up the honey-voiced drawl that was common among Southern belles in Atlanta but an exotic and appealing rarity in Michigan.

"No. I brought you some hot chocolate."

She grinned at him. "Thank you. I haven't had any in years." She reached for it as she motioned to a mug in the sand. "I fixed myself some instant coffee this mornin' 'cause I didn't know if you wanted a whole pot."

She drank coffee now. Not hot chocolate.

Heat crept up Luke's neck. "I always make a pot."

"I'll remember that. Luke, meet Jason and Eric. They were down at the public beach and wandered up this way. We were just gettin' acquainted. Jason, Eric, this is my brother, Luke."

The two guys gave him polite nods, and Jason stuck out his hand. "Nice to meet you, sir."

Although Luke was used to that title from his military days, it suddenly made him feel old.

He released the kid's hand and opened his chair. "Well, don't let me interrupt your conversation. I'll just enjoy the view." He set up his chair a few feet away, angled in their direction, rather than toward the water, and sat down.

Hannah shot him a surprised look while the two college jocks shifted on the sand, clearly uncomfortable with his presence.

Good.

The boys made stilted small talk for a couple of minutes, and then Hannah stood, shooting a disgruntled glare at Luke before addressing her admirers.

"Want to take a walk? It looks like the beach goes on for miles in that direction. And I could use some exercise after sittin' in planes for hours yesterday." She gestured down the long expanse of sand in the opposite direction of the nearby public beach, where a few family groups were gathered.

"Sure." Jason's relief was transparent.

Hannah reached down for her hot chocolate and raised it in salute to Luke. "Thanks again for this. I'll be back in a little while."

She paused for a split second, as if waiting to see whether he was going to protest—and embarrass her further.

Stymied, he stared at her in silence.

With a flip of her hair, she turned her back and sauntered down the sand, a stud on each side.

Luke blew out a frustrated breath as they walked away, the tension once more bunching in his shoulders. Talk about being blindsided. When he'd agreed to let Hannah come, he'd been worried about keeping her entertained.

That was obviously not going to be a problem.

Instead, he had a bigger one.

As he watched the threesome grow smaller in the distance, a muscle clenched in his jaw and he tightened his grip on his mug.

Lord, I think I'm going to need some help here.

From the far side of her yard, where she'd gone to retrieve a plastic shopping bag the wind had tossed into a bush, Kelsey watched the tableau below with amusement. Her view of the beach was unobstructed by leafy branches, and she didn't need sound—or subtitles—to figure out what was going on.

Nor did she have any trouble discerning Luke's frustration—and panic. Though the tall beach grass obscured details, the sudden stiffening in his stance when he'd come across the scene—and the protective placement of his beach chair—communicated loud and clear.

But he'd been one-upped by the blonde, who had to be Hannah. There'd been defiance in her stance as she'd faced off with him, and triumph in her saunter when she'd walked away with the two young men.

It looked as if Luke was going to need some help with his sister sooner rather than later.

After snagging the wayward bag off the bush, Kelsey returned to the house and gathered up her own beach things, as well as a tin of scones Dorothy had sent home with her yesterday. She kept an eye on the long stretch of sand, and when she saw Luke's sister and her admirers making their way back down the beach twenty minutes later, she headed out the door and toward the steps, picking up her own beach chair along the way.

She timed her arrival to theirs, flashing them a smile as she emerged from the tall grass. "Good morning."

Luke stood when he caught sight of her, and she waved before turning her attention back to the three younger people who had halted opposite her. "You must be Hannah, Luke's sister." She held out her hand. "I'm Kelsey, your next-door neighbor."

The girl smiled and took her hand. "Luke told me about you."

Though she kept her smile firmly fixed, Kelsey wondered what Luke had said. "I've heard about you, too. Welcome to Michigan."

Luke came up beside them. "Can I carry that for you?" He gestured toward Kelsey's bag and chair.

"Sure. Over there will be fine." She handed them to him and gestured farther down the beach. "Would you like to join me?"

She pinned him with a meaningful look, and after a moment he nodded. "Okay. I'll set you up, then get my stuff."

Hannah flashed her a grateful smile as Luke moved down the beach.

"I have some homemade scones in my bag, if you all are interested." She encompassed the small group in her comment. "Blueberry, cinnamon and lemon. Why don't you give me a minute to get set up, and then come help yourselves? I have plenty."

"Okay. Thanks." Hannah spoke for all of them.

Luke's sister headed toward her chair, and her two admirers followed as if she were the Pied Piper.

While Luke collected his things, Kelsey made her way over to her own chair and awkwardly lowered herself into it. Her neighbor was right. One of these days very soon she was going to have to switch to a regular lawn chair. She could still get into this one. But getting out was becoming a major problem.

By the time he returned and set up his chair beside

her, she had settled in and was opening the canvas bag she'd toted down with her.

"I take it I made a tactical error."

The corners of her mouth lifted into a smile at his quiet comment. "Kids that age need space."

He sighed and settled his sunglasses on his nose, all the while keeping tabs on his sister. "Yeah. But they also need supervision. Even if they don't think they do." He narrowed his eyes as one of the young men leaned in close to Hannah.

Kelsey's lips twitched. "That's true. But a more subtle approach might work better."

He transferred his attention to her. With the dark shades, she couldn't read his eyes, but she could feel his scrutiny.

"What those guys have on their minds isn't subtle."

A flush warmed her cheeks, and she made a production out of pulling the tin of scones from her bag. "Maybe not. But Hannah seems to be handling them just fine. And they appear to be behaving themselves."

"Things might be different if we weren't close by." He raked his fingers through his hair and shook his head. "I was afraid this visit might be challenging. But this wasn't the kind of challenge I had in mind."

As laughter drifted their way from the three younger people, Kelsey looked toward them and held up the tin. Hannah smiled and spoke to the young men, and the three of them started down the beach.

"You might want to give her a chance to prove she's responsible before you shift into overprotective mode." Kelsey popped the lid on the scones and held the tin out to him. "I recommend the blueberry. And I'd take one quick if I were you. I have a feeling those two young guys are going to make short work of my stash."

Ten minutes later, as Luke dug around in the bottom of the tin for the few crumbs that remained, he had to admit Kelsey had been right about Hannah's admirers. They'd devoured Dorothy's scones.

She'd been right about being overprotective, too. As Hannah interacted with the young men while they ate their scones, she was poised, confident—and in control. With every gesture and every word, she was setting clear boundaries for them. Letting them know what pleased her—and what didn't. It was masterful to watch, from the look of disapproval she shot Eric after he uttered an offensive word, to the wrinkled nose she offered Jason when he mentioned a raucous drinking party his fraternity had sponsored last school year.

As the three younger people conversed a few feet away, Kelsey raised an eyebrow at him, as if to say, *See? She's fine. You have nothing to worry about.*

He wasn't convinced of that yet, but he did feel a little less driven to hover over her every minute of her stay. Not that he could anyway, with his commitments to the youth center project. That was part of the problem.

Hannah wandered over for another scone, then made a face when she found the tin empty. "Those were great, Kelsey. Did you make them?"

"No." She closed the tin and slipped it back in her bag. "My shop mate did. She runs a tearoom."

"Yeah?" Hannah plopped onto the sand beside her. "That's cool. I'm starting to get into cooking. Do you think she'd give me the recipes for these?"

"I'll ask her for you."

"So you make quilts, right?" Hannah lifted a handful of sand and let it sift through her fingers.

"That's right."

"That's cool, too, I guess. If you're into the country look." She gave Kelsey a sheepish grin. "That's not my thing."

"It's not mine, either."

His sister furrowed her brow. "But isn't that what quilting is all about?"

"Not the kind I do. This is quilted." She hefted the tote at her side. The modern, geometric design defied every stereotype Luke had about quilting.

"For real?" Hannah examined it, running her fingers over the colorful pattern.

"Yep. Here, let me show you the pattern I'm sketching for my new commission."

As Kelsey dug into her tote bag again, Luke noticed that the two guys in the background were getting restless. Cooking and quilting were obviously not high on their list of interesting topics.

Hannah apparently came to the same realization. Excusing herself, she rose and strolled over to them. After a brief conversation, they took off down the beach and she dropped down beside Kelsey again.

"What's up with your new friends?" Luke leaned back in his chair and folded his hands over his stomach.

She shrugged. "They'll be bored with this stuff. But I'll see them around again. They'll be here for another ten days."

And with that, the two women put their heads together in an intense discussion about fabrics and designs and techniques. He heard words like "tacking" and "batting" being bandied about, but they had little meaning to him—at least in the context of quilts.

Luke tuned out the conversation, leaned his head back and let the warmth of the sun seep into his skin. As long as Hannah was with Kelsey, he could relax. Might as well take advantage of the moment.

The next thing he knew, a jab on his arm jolted him awake. Jerking upright, he gripped the edges of his chair, every muscle taut, ready to spring into action.

Hannah regarded him from a foot away, eyes wide. "Sorry, Luke. I didn't mean to scare you."

He unclenched his fingers from the arms of the chair and forced his lips into a smile. "No problem.

I guess I spent too much time on the front lines. So what have you ladies been up to while I zoned out?"

His sister switched gears at once, quickly moving past his extreme reaction. It took Kelsey a few seconds longer to regroup. As Hannah gave him a recap of their conversation, his neighbor gathered up her things and tucked them back in her tote bag, the tremble in her fingers obvious as she fumbled with the snap.

"So, would that be okay?"

At Hannah's question, he refocused on her. "What?"

"Could I visit Kelsey at her shop and meet Dorothy? The lady who made those great scones?"

"Oh. Sure. Maybe Monday, if that's okay with Kelsey."

"We'd love for you to stop by. And speaking of the shop, it's time for me to get ready for work."

She made a move to stand, and Luke rose at once to extend a hand.

Flashing him a chagrined look, she accepted it and let him pull her to her feet. "Thanks. I'm switching to the regular lawn chair for my next visit." She folded up the beach chair, tucked it under her arm and reached for her bag.

"Why don't I carry that up for you?"

"Thanks, but I can manage. It's not heavy now, since we finished off all those scones." She winked at his sister, who smiled back. "You two stay here and soak up some rays. It's a perfect beach day." With a wave, she set off for the steps.

Luke watched her go while Hannah trotted over to retrieve her beach chair. Less than half a minute later, his sister returned.

"I bet it's not easy to do all those steps if you're pregnant." Hannah checked on Kelsey, who had paused at the midway landing, while she set up her chair.

"I'm sure it's not."

"So what's her story?" Hannah plopped in her chair and tipped her head up to him. "You didn't say much yesterday, other than she was pregnant and here alone."

"That's all I know."

"Yeah? Do you think her husband died or something? I mean, a guy would have to be nuts to divorce someone like her. She's cool."

Kelsey reached the top of the steps, and Luke eased back into his own chair. He didn't disagree with Hannah's conclusion. Why a man would willingly walk away from a woman like Kelsey was beyond comprehension. From what he'd seen so far, she was smart, caring, strong and had her priorities straight. As for his sister's question about Kelsey's marital status—he had no idea.

"She's a very private person, Hannah. And I've only been here a week. It takes longer than that to establish a friendship strong enough to exchange confidences."

"Hmm." Hannah spread some sunscreen on her arms, her expression thoughtful. "I thought she was very open. I mean, she didn't have to tell me about how her sister thought she was crazy to throw away her corporate job and move here. Or how her grandmother taught her to quilt when she was a little girl, and how much she misses her. Or how she's not sleeping very well anymore because the baby kicks so much."

Dumbfounded, Luke twisted his head toward his sister. "When did she tell you all that?"

"While you were sleeping." She put down the tube of sunscreen and faced him. "So we need to have a talk, okay?"

"About what?" He was still grappling with all the information Hannah had learned about his neighbor in the space of—he checked his watch—thirty minutes.

"About being superbrother. Here's the thing, Luke—you don't have to worry about me. I know how to handle guys. You need to trust me."

"I do trust you. I'm not so sure about the guys."

"Look...I'm only going to be here three weeks. What's the point of starting something that's going nowhere? I'd rather hang around Kelsey, to be honest. All guys want to talk about is sports. Not my thing. And for the record, I don't fool around. I still go to church every Sunday, and my values are solid. So give me some space. And quit worrying, okay?"

Time for an attitude adjustment. Time to take Kelsey's advice and dial down the protective mode.

"Maybe I hovered a little too much this morning."

"Ya think?" She rolled her eyes again.

"But I promised Mom and Dad I'd watch out for you."

"I know. And I promised them I wouldn't give you any trouble about that. Unless you went overboard." She stuck out her hand. "Truce?"

A grin tugged at his lips and he took her fingers. "Truce."

She returned the smile, then closed her eyes and settled in for some serious beach time.

Luke did the same, his mind once again more at ease. He was liking this grown-up sister of his. And Kelsey obviously was, too.

An image of his neighbor struggling up the steps alone flashed across his mind, and his smile dimmed. The alone part bothered him.

But maybe, with Hannah here, he'd find out more about her solitary state. The two of them had hit it off, and she'd already told his sister more than she'd told him in a week.

Not that he intended to pry, of course. Or ask Hannah to reveal confidences. But if a few discreet questions ferreted out a nugget or two of information, he wasn't averse to asking them.

Because the more he saw of Kelsey, the more he

was convinced she carried a burden that was weighing down her slender shoulders.

And whether it was wise or not, he wanted to help her shed some of it.

Chapter Seven

Luke slipped his arms into his sports jacket and tapped on the bathroom door as he passed. "Five-minute warning."

The door opened, and Hannah poked her head out. "I need ten."

"Eight."

"Okay, okay. Why do we have to go to the early service anyway? This is supposed to be a vacation." She stifled a yawn.

"I thought it might be less crowded. We can go later next Sunday, if you'd rather. There's one at ten, too."

"I vote for that." She shut the door.

While he waited, he booted up his laptop and checked his email. Messages had been flying all week among the youth fellowship board members, and they'd hammered out a lot of the fundraising plan. At tomorrow morning's meeting, they'd finalize it and move ahead on all fronts—including implementing the communications and PR initiatives Kelsey had been tweaking for them as the plan solidified. She already had a newspaper interview lined up for him tomorrow afternoon with *The Record* in Saugatuck, and one with *The Holland Sentinel* on Wednesday.

When Hannah appeared nine minutes later, he checked his watch and arched an eyebrow.

Heaving a long-suffering sigh, she planted her hands on her hips. "Chill, big brother. It's only five after eight. How long will it take to get to church?"

"I'm not sure." He clicked his computer shut. "This will be my first visit. I was too jet-lagged last Sunday to do more than veg."

"Hmph. Good thing God doesn't veg out on *you*."

He grinned. "You sound like Mom."

She made a face at him. "Ha-ha. So let's get this show on the road."

Twelve minutes after they pulled out of their driveway, Luke angled into a parking spot beside the small, white church in Saugatuck, where Reverend Howard presided. The man had impressed him at last week's board meeting, and Luke had toyed with giving the man's church a try.

Finding out Kelsey was a congregant had clinched his decision.

Funny how his attitude about his neighbor had

done a one-eighty in the past week. When he'd found her on his beach, he'd been annoyed at the intrusion. Now he looked forward to their encounters.

Go figure.

They slipped into a pew near the back, and a few minutes before the service began Kelsey walked past them down the aisle. Alone, as usual. And so focused on the stained glass window above the sanctuary, with its soaring representation of the Resurrection, that she didn't even notice them.

He expected her to sit alone, too. But he was pleased when Dorothy waved at her and slid over to make room in her pew.

The organ music swelled, and Luke did his best to immerse himself in the service. Yet he found his gaze wandering to the blond-haired mother-to-be far too often. A nudge in the side from Hannah's elbow after he skipped a verse in one of the hymns helped him refocus.

As he'd expected, Reverend Howard's sermon was excellent—and appropriate to the day's reading from Matthew, about Peter's faltering trust as he walked toward the Lord across the water.

"How often in our lives have circumstances overwhelmed us and undermined our faith?" the pastor concluded. "How often, in the midst of crises, does our trust in the Lord waver and we, like Peter, begin to sink? Not into water, but into despair and desperation and depression?

"My friends, the message of today's reading is

simple. No matter what perils befall us…no matter how many bad things happen to us…no matter how alone or lost we feel…the Lord is always nearby, His hand outstretched, waiting to save us if we but ask. Waiting to banish our fears. So be not afraid. Go to Him in your need, and He will never fail you."

The organist played the introduction to Carlos's favorite hymn, "Amazing Grace," and Luke opened his hymnal. No matter the danger, no matter the risk, the young medic had never been afraid.

"The Lord called me to this work," he'd once confided as they'd shared a meal during a rare quiet interlude, when Luke had asked about his steady calmness under fire. "This is where I belong. And if He calls me home while I'm here…" The man had shrugged. "His will be done."

"But what about all your plans?" Luke had pressed. "Being a paramedic, having a family of your own, the youth center…."

Carlos had just smiled. "The Lord's plans trump mine any day." And then he'd snatched Luke's cookie off his tray and popped it in his mouth with a grin, lightening the serious mood.

The man's joy, his trust, his confidence, had infused Luke's heart with new fervor for the Lord. And had banished many of his own fears—and regrets.

But not all of them.

Swallowing past the lump in his throat, Luke dropped out of the song. He felt Hannah send him a questioning glance, but he ignored her as he struggled to rein in his emotions.

Funny. In the field, he'd had no trouble keeping an iron grip on his feelings. There, it had been a matter of survival. As it was, every young life lost had ripped at his gut. Had he given in fully to the pain, he wouldn't have been able to function.

Now, back in safe territory, his emotions were straining at the tight leash he'd kept them on for years. Especially his feelings about Carlos.

The man who had saved his life.

Carlos had never agreed with him on that point, always countering by saying he hadn't known there was a sniper on the roof when he'd tugged Luke back into the shelter of the mud hut where they'd taken refuge. He'd just wanted to ask his advice about one of the wounded soldiers he was treating. *You should thank God, not me,* he'd later told Luke. *It was His hand, not a human one, that saved you.*

All Luke knew was that the next man out of the hut had taken a fatal bullet in the brain.

Three weeks later, Carlos, too, had died.

The young medic's final words echoed in his mind. *Let not your heart be troubled.*

Good advice. But hard to follow.

And Luke had a strong suspicion his neighbor, seated a dozen pews in front of him—her blond hair spotlighted by a shaft of morning light radiating through the stained glass window in the sanctuary— felt the same way.

"Hey."

At the whispered word, he looked over at Hannah.

"You okay?"

He nodded and picked up the melody as they came to one of his favorite lines. "T'was grace that brought us safe thus far, and grace will lead us home."

Give me that grace, Lord. And please give it to Kelsey, too.

Kelsey saw Luke and Hannah as soon as she exited the church. They were off to one side of the lawn, chatting with Reverend Howard.

Her step faltered, causing the man on her heels to run into her.

With a mumbled apology, she moved out of the line of traffic, keeping her neighbor and his sister in sight.

Since parting from the two of them on the beach yesterday morning, their paths hadn't crossed. But she'd heard their laughter on the deck last night. Smelled the aroma of barbecue as she'd prepared her solitary meal and placed her weekly call to her sister. Seen the flicker of candlelight on their patio table as she'd eaten her baked chicken breast on the screened porch and paged through the latest issue of *Quilting Arts.*

It was her typical Saturday night ritual. And it suited her fine.

Or it had, until last night.

For the first time since coming to Michigan and moving into the cozy, memory-filled house that still seemed infused with Gram's presence, she'd felt lonely.

And she didn't want to feel lonely. Didn't want to start thinking about all the things she lacked, when the Lord had blessed her with so much.

Someday…maybe…she'd meet a man—perhaps a man a lot like Luke—whose love would fill her life with warmth and whose steady presence and gentle patience would put her nightmares to rest once and for all.

But Luke wasn't that man. Because while it was possible he had the qualifications for the part, he wasn't going to be around long enough to play it.

As she struggled to contain a throat-tightening surge of melancholy, Reverend Howard shifted toward her. With a smile, he raised his hand and beckoned.

Too bad. She'd have preferred to escape unnoticed to her car.

But there was no way she could ignore the minister's summons without being rude. Resigned, she smoothed down the front of her dress, joined the throng of people descending the steps and crossed the lawn.

Hannah looked stunning this morning, just as she had on the beach yesterday, her mane of blond hair dazzling in the sun, her youthful face lit up in welcome.

But as she approached the threesome, it was Luke who captured her attention.

Like the day he'd visited her shop, he was dressed in a sports coat that sat well on his broad shoulders, this one navy blue. A few springy dark hairs peeked out through the open neck of his blue-striped dress shirt. His tan slacks were pressed and creased, his shoes polished to a high gloss, his dark hair neatly combed.

No question about it. Captain Luke Turner was one handsome man.

Tall, too. He towered over her by a good eight inches. Yet she no longer felt fear in his presence. And that was good.

But the little flutter of attraction that danced along her nerve endings when he smiled at her wasn't.

"Good morning, Kelsey." Reverend Howard cocooned her hand in both of his. "We were just talking about the youth center, and we wanted to get your opinion about an idea Luke had. Why don't you explain it?" The pastor turned to the man at his side.

"To be honest, it's Hannah's idea." Luke tossed his sister a grin. "I was explaining the project to her over dinner last night, and she suggested we set up a Twitter page for the project. She thinks it could be a way to get information about it to a much wider audience."

Kelsey nodded. "I like the notion of using social

media to help spread the word. It has no geographic or demographic limitations."

"I could set it up for you while I'm here," Hannah offered. "It's not hard to do. And I could post updates even after I go home. We could use it to direct people to the website for the project and keep them updated on developments. It's kind of a cool way to participate in a worthwhile cause. And I have to do a service project during senior year anyway. I know this would qualify."

"Sold." Kelsey smiled and shot Luke a quick glance. *Nothing to worry about with this young woman,* she telegraphed.

One side of his mouth twitched, telling her he'd received the message.

"Excellent, excellent." Reverend Howard beamed at them. "We'll have a final fundraising plan after tomorrow's meeting, and then we can really get this thing rolling. Father Joe will be ecstatic. As we all are, of course. What a blessing you've been to us, Luke." He clapped the army doctor on the shoulder.

A ruddy tinge crept over Luke's face, and he gave a dismissive shrug. "Carlos is the one who deserves thanks. If he hadn't been so inspiring—and so passionate about this project—I wouldn't be here."

"Well…blessings come in many ways and many forms." The pastor encompassed all of them with a sunny smile. "Now I see Harriet Lucas waving at me. I need to ask how her husband is doing since his

knee replacement surgery. I'll talk to you all soon."
Lifting his hand in farewell, he set off across the
lawn.

Kelsey adjusted the strap of her purse and shifted
her weight from one foot to the other. "I think I'll
be off, too. Are you planning to put in some more
beach time?"

She directed the question to both of them, but
Hannah answered.

"Not today. We're going to have brunch, and then
Luke's going to show me around Saugatuck. Would
you like to join us?"

Luke's expression told Kelsey he was as taken
aback by the impromptu invitation as she was.

"I'm not exactly shod for doing a lot of walking."
She gestured to her inch-and-a-half-heel dress shoes.
"Now if I had my Nikes…"

"Why don't you at least eat with us? It's okay, isn't
it, Luke?" Hannah turned to her brother.

A quick peek told Kelsey he'd recovered from
his initial surprise. Now he looked receptive to the
idea.

More than receptive.

"Absolutely. In fact, maybe you can make a recommendation for a good spot."

He smiled, and the warmth in his eyes set off a
little quiver in the pit of her stomach.

Get a grip, Kelsey. He's asking advice about a
place to eat, not asking you out on a date.

She took a deep breath. "Pumpernickel's downtown is nice, if you're after a casual, relaxed atmosphere. They have a lovely porch, and the cinnamon rolls are great."

"Sounds perfect. Shall we follow you there, or would you like to ride with us?"

Had she said she was going? She didn't think so. But he was acting as if she had. He'd already linked arms with Hannah and was waiting for her response.

Fine. She liked Pumpernickel's. Hannah would be with them. It would be a nice, casual breakfast.

"Uh…follow me, I guess."

"Great." He flashed her another smile and followed as she led the way to the parking lot.

Saugatuck was small, and the drive took less than five minutes, even with tourist traffic. Finding a parking place, however, took a lot longer. She motioned out her window to the restaurant as she passed it, leaving them on their own to locate a spot for their car.

Ten minutes and three blocks later, she puffed up to the main door on foot to find them waiting for her.

"You should have ridden with us. Someone was pulling out right in front when we doubled back." Hannah motioned to Luke's white rental Camry, ten feet away.

It figured.

But driving on her own had felt safer.

"At least I got my exercise for the day. Shall we go in?"

Luke held the door, and their chairs, in true Southern gentleman fashion. As she settled into her seat, Kelsey couldn't help noticing that the tall, toned, dark-haired doctor drew more than his share of interested glances from the women customers. She kept that observation to herself, but Hannah didn't.

"Man, you are getting the once-over from every female in this place," his sister teased him.

The tips of Luke's ears reddened, and Kelsey stifled a grin. For a moment, she was tempted to tease him, too. But he seemed embarrassed enough already. Which was kind of cute. And endearing. Vanity was clearly not one of his faults.

"Do you have any brothers, Kelsey?" Hannah spread her napkin on her lap.

Giving him a reprieve, Kelsey turned her attention to the young woman beside her. "No brothers. Just the one older sister I mentioned yesterday. But thanks to her, I have two darling nephews and a sweet little niece. The boys are six and nine, and Emily is four. She's a doll. Would you like to see a picture of them?"

"Sure."

As Kelsey searched through her purse, she took a sidelong look at Luke. The pink in his ears was beginning to fade.

Pulling out her wallet, she flipped through the

plastic sleeves. "This is my favorite. It's from last Christmas."

She turned it around and passed it over to Hannah. Luke leaned close to examine it, too. In the shot, her sister and brother-in-law sat on the floor by their fireplace, their smiling children clustered around them.

"They look like a nice family. Where do they live?" Hannah handed the wallet back.

"Dallas. That's where I grew up."

"I thought you lived in St. Louis before you came here?" Luke shot her a quizzical look.

"My job took me there." She tucked the wallet back into her purse.

Hannah fiddled with the straw in her water glass. "It's too bad the cousins will live so far from each other."

The innocent remark reminded Kelsey yet again that she had a choice to make. And depending on what she decided, the cousins might never know each other.

That thought saddened her.

The waitress arrived, saving her from having to respond. But after they placed their orders, she caught Luke watching her. And she continued to feel his surreptitious scrutiny throughout the meal. As she picked at her Huevos Pumpernickel, a dish she usually demolished, she tried to smile and chat as if everything was fine. But she sensed Luke had detected her sudden change of mood—and knew she was troubled.

Much to her relief, the conversation remained on impersonal topics for the rest of the meal. Nevertheless, she was glad when sufficient time passed for her to leave without appearing rude.

Taking one last bite of egg, she wiped her lips and used the napkin to hide the substantial amount of food that remained on her plate.

"Well, I need to be off. I have some errands to run, including a trip to the grocery store." She stood.

Luke rose, too. "I thought I'd drop Hannah off at your shop in the morning, on my way to the board meeting. She can look around and visit with Ms. Martin, if that's okay. Around nine forty-five?"

"That's fine." She smiled at Hannah. "I told Dorothy about you, by the way, and she's looking forward to meeting you."

"Great. Maybe I can even get her to share those scone recipes."

"I have absolute confidence you'll charm them right out of her. Thank you both for inviting me today."

"It was our pleasure." The warmth was back in Luke's eyes. Along with questions.

She tried to ignore both.

Picking up her purse, she aimed a smile their way, then wound through the diners to the street, passing a large table where a group ranging in age from seniors to toddlers was laughing and chatting.

Most likely an extended family that had convened in the Saugatuck area for a vacation or a reunion. It happened all the time around here.

As she walked past the happy family, one of the young children darted from his seat to chase a wayward fork. She pulled up short, placing a protective hand on her stomach while the mother apologized and pulled the toddler out of her path.

The baby kicked under her fingers, perhaps protesting the abrupt halt, and a smile tugged at her lips. Day by day, the child within her grew more active—and assertive. And day by day, her emotional investment in the new life she was carrying intensified.

Yet Reverend Howard was right. Every child deserved to be cherished with a love that was free of baggage and untainted by bad memories.

Unfortunately, she had plenty of both.

As she trekked toward her car, she once again wrestled with the questions that increasingly plagued her. When she held her baby for the first time, would her heart fill with love—or antipathy? Would she experience joy and contentment—or be reminded of pain and terror and revulsion?

She didn't know. Yet.

But she prayed every day for enlightenment.

And she also prayed for courage. To not only make the right decision, but to see it through.

Wherever that might lead her.

Chapter Eight

Luke angled his car into a spot across from Kelsey's shop, set the brake and noted the time on the old-fashioned clock that held a place of honor on Douglas's quaint main thoroughfare. Twelve-fifteen. The board meeting had run a full two hours; he hoped Hannah hadn't worn out her welcome—or gotten bored.

But three minutes later, when he stepped inside the shop, he found her bustling around the tearoom, a smile on her face as she helped serve lunch.

Spotting him, she waved and strode over, the frilly white apron with starched ruffles at the shoulders looking incongruous over her stone-washed jeans and pink tank top.

"Hi, Luke. How was the meeting?"

"Good." He gestured to her attire. "What's this all about?"

She smoothed the crisp white fabric over her jeans. "Dorothy was in a bind. She only has two servers, and one of them quit without any notice this morning. Since Dorothy had just shared her scone recipes with me, I offered to pitch in. Seemed like a fair exchange. And you know what? I'm having a blast!"

One of the patrons at a nearby table raised her hand, and Hannah called out to her. "I'll be right with ya'll." Then she gave him a hug. "Gotta go. You don't mind if I hang around here this afternoon, do you? Kelsey said she'd give me a ride home when the shop closes at four. And she said I could sit in on her beginners quilting class at two-thirty."

"Sure. That's fine." So much for his worries about her being bored.

"You want some lunch? The asparagus quiche is to die for, and it comes with lemon scones and a strawberry salad. There's homemade apple cobbler for dessert, too, if you're still hungry. Warm from the oven. With ice cream."

"Okay. You convinced me. I'll stop in and see Kelsey for a minute first, though. Is she here?" He scanned the quilt shop, but didn't see any sign of her.

"She was." Hannah looked over her shoulder. "But she told me she likes to walk to the lake at lunch. Maybe she went down there. Or she might be in the back room. You can check."

Without waiting for a response, she hurried over to the customer who had summoned her.

Left on his own, Luke strolled into the Not Your

Grandmother's Quilts side of the shop, checking out Kelsey's home away from home. On his first visit, he'd been so surprised to discover his neighbor was the PR expert recommended by Reverend Howard that he'd hardly noticed his surroundings. And she'd whisked him over to Tea for Two before he'd had a chance to look around her shop.

As he wandered through the merchandise, the conversation he'd overheard between his sister and Kelsey on the beach Saturday came back to him. Now he understood what she'd meant when she told Hannah she didn't do country. The quilts on display were more like modern art, featuring swirls of color, geometric patterns and 3-D designs. That same artsy look could also be found in the smaller items on display—wall hangings of various sizes, purses, tote bags, table runners, placemats, pot holders, pillow covers. The designs were eye-catching and created with impressive flair.

No question about it, the shop definitely lived up to its name. These quilts were nothing like the homespun version favored by his Grandma Turner, who'd made a quilt or two in her day. He could see why Hannah had found them appealing. And why she was intrigued enough to want to take a class.

Venturing farther back, he noted the work table he'd spotted on his first visit, and the desk with the computer where Kelsey had been working that day. In the opposite corner, a partly finished quilt in shades of blue, green and magenta was secured in a stand-alone quilting frame, the intricate design stunning. A swivel lamp was attached to the frame, and an adjustable chair on rollers was pushed underneath. Bolts of fabric were tucked into shelves along the back wall, and two sewing machines stood at the ready.

As Luke finished his tour, the bell over the front door jingled. He turned in time to see Kelsey enter.

She saw him at once, hesitating for a fraction of a second before she moved into the shop. "Hi. Have you been here long?"

"Less than five minutes. Sorry I'm so late. The meeting ran long."

"No problem." She deposited her oversized tote—the one Hannah had admired at the beach—on the work table. "Is everything a go?"

"Yes. Plus, I have other good news. Father Joe met with Steve Lange, who owns the property the board has its eye on for the center, and managed to sweet-talk him into agreeing to sell the land to the youth fellowship for less than its book value and take the rest as a charitable donation."

Kelsey smiled. "I have to meet this dynamo padre one of these days."

"There's more. Dennis Lawson, the manager of the hotel where Carlos worked in high school, offered to host the fundraising dinner and auction at cost. And one of the other pastors has an award-winning architect in his congregation who may be willing to comp his design services for the center." He grinned. "Not bad for a week's work."

She leaned back against the edge of the work table and folded her arms across her chest. "That's an understatement. And Father Joe and his colleagues aren't the only ones with silver tongues. You roped me into the project, too. Quite a feat."

He didn't know how to interpret that last remark, and she continued without giving him time to decipher it.

"Hannah says she'll bring her computer in here tomorrow and work on the Twitter idea, since I have wireless. I've also contacted the TV news programs in Holland and Grand Rapids. They sound interested in doing a story. And I think it would be helpful if you visit the churches that sponsor the youth fellowship and make a personal pitch. It would probably take you three Sundays to hit them all, but it's doable if you're willing. I checked the times of services at all of them. Part of your pitch should involve soliciting donations for the dinner auction—and encouraging people to attend. This kind of event can bring in big bucks if enough publicity and support is generated. Are you ready for this afternoon's interview?"

Head reeling from her rapid-fire delivery, he nodded. "I think so."

"Did you prepare any talking points?"

"I thought I'd just answer the reporter's questions."

She shook her head. "Not good enough. You have to guide the interview. No matter what you're asked, no matter what the reporter's agenda, you have to make sure you get *your* message out." Pushing up from the table, she moved over to her desk, plucked up a printed sheet and handed it to him.

He skimmed the bullet points, impressed. In a few lines, she'd captured the key messages he needed to convey to the media, the congregations and any other groups he might address. The who, what, where, why and how were all laid out for him, with suggestions for ways to give the story the kind of emotional appeal that would tug at the heartstrings—and persuade people to open their wallets.

"This is great." He looked up. "Hannah suggested I have lunch at the tearoom, so I'll study this while I eat and jot down some notes." He shot her an admiring look as he folded the sheet of paper in half. "I have a feeling you left a big hole in your company when you walked away."

She gave a rueful shake of her head. "In the corporate world, no one is missed for long. Besides, I prefer to apply my skills to my own business. Although it took a—" She stopped. Moistened her lips. "…a strong wake-up call for me to realize I'd rather make my mark in my own business than in someone else's."

"What kind of wake-up call?" He knew it was a gamble to ask. She'd been skittish and close-mouthed around him since they'd met. Yet she'd seemed relaxed around Hannah, shared some of her history with his sister. Maybe she felt comfortable enough with him by now to answer that question.

Wrong.

"Long story." She brushed him off with a wave of her hand and moved on. "Anyway, I'm doing a major overhaul of my grandmother's website, and I'll be targeting very specific media with story ideas that should generate orders for the shop."

Okay. Fine. She wanted to stick to business, he'd stick to business.

And try not to let it bother him that she was willing to talk to Hannah but not to him.

"That sounds like it may be very effective. But how much can one person produce?"

"It depends. Custom-designed, hand-sewn quilts like that one—" she gestured to the in-progress blue-and-green number he'd noticed earlier "—are very high-end, very time-consuming...and very expensive. My grandmother used the income from them to supplement her Social Security, but I need to earn a living. So I also do machine-quilted commissions. And I've turned lots of my designs into smaller items that could even be outsourced and mass-produced." She gestured to the sheet of paper in his hand. "Now you'd better start prepping. The interview is in an hour and a half. Where are you meeting the reporter?"

"At St. Francis."

"Good choice. Have him get a few quotes from Father Joe, too, if you can."

"Luke." Hannah hissed at him from between two of the quilts that separated the shops. "Are you eating here or not? We're down to our last piece of asparagus quiche."

"I'll be right over."

"Okay." Her head disappeared and the quilts fell back into place.

He refocused on Kelsey. "It sounds like my sister has made herself at home here. She mentioned sitting in on a quilting class this afternoon."

"Yes. It's a beginner class that will meet every afternoon this week. By Friday, everyone will have designed and stitched a small wall hanging. If she decides to continue to help at Tea for Two, the timing will work out great. And you won't have to worry about who she's with. Or what she's doing."

"I think I've gotten past that."

"I'm sure Hannah will be relieved." Kelsey's mouth twitched, drawing his attention to her lips.

With an effort, he dragged his gaze back to her eyes. Some wariness still lurked in their depths, but a flash of humor gave him an intriguing peek at her playful side. He'd spotted it for a moment yesterday, too, when Hannah had ribbed him at Pumpernickel's about drawing admiring glances. Kelsey had seemed poised to join in the fun, but then she'd backed off. At the time, he'd been grateful. Now, he wished she'd followed her instincts. He had a feeling he'd have enjoyed being teased by her.

And this line of thought was not going to help him prepare for the interview.

He lifted his hand and waved the paper. "Wish me luck."

"You'll do fine. Just speak from the heart."

"Right."

Retracing his steps to the front of the shop, he crossed into Tea for Two and let Hannah show him to a table. As he ate his meal and jotted notes on the sheet Kelsey had prepared for him, he replayed her final instruction in his mind.

Speak from the heart.

It might not be easy, but he could do that. This was his final, self-imposed mission, and he didn't intend to fail. Letting Carlos down wasn't an option. If he had to reach deep for the emotions locked in his heart, he'd do so. The outcome mattered too much to let his usual self-contained manner and self-control get in the way.

And there was another outcome that mattered, too—finding out what made his wary neighbor tick.

But he was far less clear on his motivation for *that* mission.

"Today was so cool, Luke!"

As he spread mayo on their turkey sandwiches, Luke smiled at Hannah while she put the cutlery and condiments on a tray. "My sister, the waitress. And here I thought you wanted to be a lawyer."

"Very funny." She wrinkled her nose and pointed a fork at him. "Dorothy is great, and I had a lot of fun. Tomorrow she said she'd let me bake a batch of the scones and give me tips along the way." She set the fork on the table, and her tone grew melancholy. "You know, she kind of reminds me of Grandma Turner."

His father's mother had died three years ago, and while her passing had saddened Luke, he'd never had the relationship with her Hannah had enjoyed. Margaret Turner had moved in with the family six years ago from her home in North Carolina, and from everything his mother had told him, she and Hannah had hit it off from the beginning.

Kind of like Kelsey and her grandmother had, from what he'd been able to discern.

And speaking of Kelsey…

Luke cut the two sandwiches in half and set them on plates, adding some potato salad he'd picked up at the deli in the grocery store on his way home from the interview. "I know you miss Grandma, Hannah. But I'm glad you like Ms. Martin. Kelsey seems to have adopted her as a grandmother, too. So how did the quilting class go?" Not the smoothest or most empathetic segue. But it would have to do.

"It was fun. I never thought I was all that artistic, but Kelsey worked with me and we came up with a great design. It will look fabulous in my room at home. She was really good with the other three ladies in the class, too. What a nice person." She added napkins to the tray and began filling glasses with water. "I can't believe she never got married. You'd think the guys would be flocking around her. But she said she was always too busy with her career to think about romance."

Luke stared at his sister. "Kelsey's never been married?"

"No."

"How do you know?"

"I asked."

"You *asked?* Just like that?"

She shot him a "get real" look. "Hey, give me some credit, okay? I'm not that tactless. I asked if she was a widow."

Better. But not by much. "Don't you think she'd have told you that if she wanted you to know?"

Setting the glasses of water on the tray, Hannah propped her hands on her hips. "My dear brother, if you don't ask questions, people think you're not interested in them. She wasn't offended, if that's what you're worried about."

"Good." He angled toward the sink on the pretense of rinsing his hands, and strove for a casual tone. "So, if she's not a widow, where's the baby's father?"

Hannah picked up the tray and headed for the back door. "I don't know. All she said was that he wasn't part of her life. That's when I stopped asking questions." She pushed the door open with her hip, walked across the deck and began unloading the tray on the glass-topped table.

As he added a small bunch of grapes to each plate, Luke mulled over this latest piece of news. It didn't add up. When they'd first met, he thought Kelsey might have been in an abusive relationship with a husband or boyfriend. The scar would suggest that.

But now that he'd gotten to know her a little, had heard Reverend Howard sing her praises, had glimpsed her strong faith, that seemed less likely. She didn't strike him as someone who would put up with abuse.

Perhaps she'd had other problems that had led her to make a mistake, though. She'd been in a high-pressure job, and she'd been focused on climbing the corporate ladder. Had she turned to drugs or alcohol to help her cope with the stress and the demands? And while under the influence of one of those, had she had a lapse in judgment that had produced this pregnancy? Was that the wake-up call she'd referred to earlier today?

An unwanted pregnancy could certainly account for her ambivalent feelings about the baby she was carrying. Yet from what he could see, she was doing all the right things to protect the health of her unborn child.

"Are you coming, Luke?" Hannah pushed open the back door and gave him a questioning look.

"Yeah. I'm on my way."

He picked up their plates and headed for the deck, more confused than ever about Kelsey Anderson.

And doubly determined to ferret out his mystery neighbor's secrets.

Chapter Nine

Kelsey stared in the bathroom mirror and sighed as she dried her hands on a paper towel. Though she'd done her best this morning, there was no disguising the bruise-like shadows beneath her eyes, the fine lines of tension at the corners of her mouth or her pallor. That's what two weeks' worth of fitful slumber could do to a person.

When she'd discussed her sleep problems with Dr. Evans yesterday, however, her OB hadn't been too concerned. In fact, the doctor had pronounced both her and the baby in good health, though Kelsey hadn't gained as much weight as expected. Even if she did feel huge.

Resigned to her wan appearance, she tossed the paper towel into the trash, tucked her hair behind her ear and headed back out front to wrap up the final session of her five-day introduction-to-quilting course. Juggling the class and a behind-schedule quilt commission with the PR work for the fast-track youth center project had been taxing, and she was glad the week was coming to an end. But all of her students had been eager and interested, and their enthusiasm had reenergized her. At least for an hour and a half a day.

As she emerged into the shop, she saw Luke hovering in the background. Her heart tripped into double time as he flashed her a smile, and she lifted a hand in response. An *unsteady* hand. The very reaction that had convinced her to follow Dorothy's advice and set up an appointment for tonight with Dr. Walters. Her handsome neighbor was bothering her way too much.

She exchanged a few words with each of her students, smiling her thanks as they showered her with praise and departed one by one. When only Hannah was left, Luke came forward.

They'd talked a few times during the week, to hammer out details on interviews and speaking engagements, but there'd been no impromptu trips for brunch. No shared beach time. Hannah had told her Luke hadn't had a minute to himself. When he wasn't doing interviews or speaking to civic groups, he was busy meeting with potential benefactors and helping with details for the dinner/auction, which would be held a few nights before he left.

In other words, he was doing what he'd come here to do. Focusing on his mission.

But she'd missed seeing him.

Yet another reason to make an appointment with Dr. Walters.

She edged behind the work table as he approached. "Sorry I couldn't give Hannah a ride home tonight, as usual."

He stopped a few feet away. "No problem. It was nice to have an excuse to stop by."

Why?

Their gazes locked, and for a moment she was afraid she'd voiced that question. Flustered, she broke eye contact and picked at a piece of lint on her shirt, searching desperately for something to say.

In the silence, Hannah looked from her to Luke—and back again.

The expression on the young woman's face went from perplexed to surprised to smug in a heartbeat, and Kelsey narrowed her eyes. She knew what Hannah was thinking. And Luke's sister was way off base. There was no potential for romance here. No way. No how.

To prove that, she summoned up her brisk corporate voice. "So, how did today's interview go?"

Luke arched an eyebrow at her business-like tone. "Very well. It's supposed to air tonight on the six o'clock news."

"Did you mention the Twitter page?" Hannah turned her attention to Luke.

"Yes. And the website Father Joc set up."

"Good. Because since you talked about it on the

radio interview Wednesday, Carlos has attracted more than a hundred followers. The TV spot should raise the numbers a lot more. Hopefully some of them will also check out the official website and send a few bucks."

"We'll take every one we can get. You ready to go?"

"Not until the grand unveiling." Hannah grinned at Luke and tapped her framed wall hanging, which lay face down on the work table.

He smiled and folded his arms across his chest. "Okay. Lay it on me."

With a flourish, she lifted the piece and turned it around. "Ta-da!"

Luke gave the modernistic rising-sun motif an appreciative scan. "I'm impressed. Didn't you tell me once you couldn't draw a straight line?"

A soft flush suffused Hannah's cheeks. "I had a lot of help with my design. Kelsey smoothed out the rough edges. And trust me, there were plenty. After that, it was just a matter of tracing the pattern, cutting out the pieces and stitching them up. Although I needed some help with the stitching part, too."

"You did great." Kelsey moved beside Hannah and put an arm around her shoulders. "Best of all, you found out there's more to the art of quilting than patchwork."

"For sure." She slid the finished piece into a plastic bag and slung her purse over her shoulder. "Okay,

I'm ready. Are you going to the beach tomorrow morning before you open the shop, Kelsey?"

"Yes. For a little while."

Kelsey was tempted to ask Luke his plans, but held back. He'd be gone in four short weeks. It wasn't wise to encourage social interaction. Besides, once he knew her story, he might lose whatever interest Hannah had picked up on a few minutes ago. Especially when he found out what she was considering doing with the baby.

"Good. We'll be there, too," Hannah told her. "You *are* going tomorrow, aren't you, Luke?"

"Yes. It doesn't make sense to stay in a beach house if you never go to the beach."

Maybe she wouldn't go, after all.

As if reading her mind, Luke pinned her with an intent look. "Why don't I carry your things down for you? About nine?"

No way would she commit to that. She might change her mind at the last minute. "I can manage. I'll only have my chair tomorrow."

Tucking her arm in her brother's, Hannah tugged him toward the door. "Let's go, Luke. Kelsey needs to leave. 'Night, Kelsey. We'll see you tomorrow."

With that, she looked back, grinned and winked.

Oh, brother.

Sinking back against the work table as the door jingled shut behind them, Kelsey shook her head. The last thing she needed was a teenage matchmaker whose head was filled with visions of romance. Yes, there were vibes between her and Luke. But she wasn't ready to deal with feelings of attraction for anyone, let alone a man who would soon be exiting her life. Besides, she had other more pressing issues to deal with before she tackled romance.

She stood, retrieved her purse from the desk and called out a good-bye to Dorothy, who was in the back baking for Saturday's customers.

It was definitely time to talk to Dr. Walters.

Luke settled behind the wheel of the car, keeping one eye on Kelsey's shop, in case she exited while they were still there. "Are you up for pizza again tonight?"

As he fumbled the key in the lock, finally looking down to slide it in, a chuckle was Hannah's only response.

He turned the key and put the car in gear. "What kind of answer is that?"

"It's not an answer. It's a reaction." She buckled her seat belt and settled her wall hanging in her lap.

"To what?"

"You."

Luke frowned as he backed out. After giving Not Your Grandmother's Quilts a final once-over, he headed down West Center toward Blue Star Highway. "I have no idea what you're talking about."

"I know. That's what's so funny."

"You want to clue me in?"

"Sure. You think Kelsey's hot."

He jerked his head toward her. "What?"

"You heard me. Watch the road." She gestured out the front window.

He made a quick course correction to avoid taking out a curbside planter.

"And on top of that, she thinks you're hot. So what are you going to do about it?"

Blindsided, he tightened his grip on the wheel and tried to regroup. "That came out of left field, didn't it?"

Although he did his best to hide his discomfiture under an amused tone, Hannah wasn't buying.

"Maybe. But I hit a home run."

"You're nuts."

"And you're avoiding the issue."

"There isn't any issue."

She chuckled again. "And they say teenagers are immature."

Irritated, he pulled onto the highway and headed for the interstate that would take them back to Pier Cove. "This has nothing to do with maturity. Yes, Kelsey is an attractive woman. But for your information, she and I got off to a very rocky start. She was not happy to discover she had to share her private beach with me. I doubt we'd even be talking if the youth center project hadn't forced us to interact."

"Then that's another blessing to come out of this project, isn't it?"

In his peripheral vision, he noticed that his knuckles were turning white on the wheel. He unclenched his fingers. "Hannah, even if there was a spark of attraction on either side—and I'm not admitting there is—it's too complicated. I'm leaving in a month. And she's pregnant."

"So? If you're in love, you can overcome the distance problem. And I thought you liked kids."

"I do."

She lifted one shoulder. "Ready-made family."

He pulled into the entrance ramp for I-196 and accelerated, his grip once more tightening on the wheel. "You're jumping to a lot of wrong conclusions."

"About what? That you're in love? Or that you could accept a child who wasn't your own?"

Man, she wasn't cutting him any slack.

"First of all, I'm not in love with Kelsey. I just met her two weeks ago. Falling in love with someone that fast would be foolish. And as for accepting a child who isn't my own...it's not a subject I've ever considered. It would depend on the circumstances. And if I *was* interested in Kelsey, her circumstances are mysterious, to say the least."

She skewered him with a look that was way too grown-up and insightful for a seventeen-year-old.

"You don't choose who to fall in love with, or how fast it happens. And I'm not saying you're there yet. But trust me, the mutual attraction is obvious. I bet even Dorothy's picked up on it. As for Kelsey's circumstances, they may be mysterious. But I've spent a lot of time with her this week, and she's a wonderful person. You could do worse. And maybe if you gave it a chance, showed you were interested in her life and had feelings for her, she might let you in on this mystery that has you so worried."

Her rebuttal finished, she settled back in her seat and turned her attention to the passing scenery.

In the silence that followed, Luke tried without much success to absorb all the implications of Hannah's little speech.

But one thing was very clear.

He'd just been lectured on romance by his kid sister.

Even worse, now that she'd brought up the subject, he doubted she was going to let it die.

Meaning he'd better get a handle on his feelings for Kelsey. Quick. And then decide what to do about them.

Before Hannah decided to step in and take charge.

Something was up.

As Kelsey emerged from the tall grass on Saturday morning and joined Luke and Hannah on the beach, she caught the warning look sent from brother to sister.

A new dynamic was at play here.

One that made her uneasy.

"Good morning." She forced her lips into a smile

and tried to read their expressions. Hannah appeared happy, relaxed and…smug was the word that came to mind. By contrast, twin furrows creased Luke's brow, and his posture was stiff as he stood to greet her.

"Hi, Kelsey." Hannah reached for the jacket on the sand beside her chair. "Did you sleep any better last night?"

Kelsey shot her a surprised look. She'd only mentioned her sleep problems once, and Hannah hadn't brought them up since. Why now?

She switched her attention to Luke. His frown had deepened, and she shifted under his scrutiny. He was a doctor. He wasn't going to miss the dark circles under her eyes, despite her efforts to camouflage them. "I think it goes with the territory." She kept her tone light as she placed a hand on her stomach. "Junior must be starting to feel confined."

"Is it a boy?" Luke moved closer, tugged her folding chair from her fingers and settled it securely in the sand beside his.

"I don't know." She tightened her grip on her mug, trying to maintain her light tone. "There's a lot to be said for being surprised, don't you think?" She lowered herself into the lawn chair as he held it steady.

Without commenting, Luke retook his seat in the low-slung beach chair.

"So what color scheme are you using in the nursery, if you don't know the baby's gender?"

At Hannah's question, Kelsey's stomach twisted, curdling the milk she'd been drinking. How in the world had they gotten on this subject?

"I'm not that far along with my plans yet. Yellow is always a safe color, though. Or green. I have a few more weeks to think about it. And things at the shop will be quieter once the summer crowd leaves. I'll have more time to focus on details like that."

Stop babbling, Kelsey. That will only arouse suspicion.

Too late. When she peeked at Luke, he was watching her from under hooded lids.

Stretching, Hannah stood, put on her jacket and gestured down the beach. "I think I'll take a little walk." With a pointed glance at her brother, she sauntered down the sand.

Kelsey couldn't see his face as he watched his sister walk away, but she was picking up some odd vibes. Like he was…nervous, maybe. Or uncertain. Odd. He'd always struck her as confident and in control and…decisive.

For some strange reason, his discomfiture had a calming effect on her. Leveled the playing field in some way. And his uncharacteristic awkwardness also made it easier to deal with Dr. Walters's recommendation. When Kelsey had explained how her initial fear of him had given way to attraction, the therapist had suggested she let those feelings surface. Not necessarily act on them, but feel them in a safe context so she'd learn not to fear them.

This was about as safe as she was going to get.

Wriggling down into her chair, she waited Luke out.

Half a minute passed before he transferred his attention from Hannah to her. When he found her watching him, his neck reddened and he groped for his sunglasses—unnecessary at this hour of the morning, with the sun at their backs.

He was hiding behind them. Just as she'd hidden behind hers at their first meeting.

Interesting.

"Hannah told me you saw your OB this week. I noticed you've been looking tired. Is everything okay?"

Whoa!

That personal comment wasn't at all what she'd expected.

Her defenses slammed back into place with the resounding clang of a prison lockdown.

"Yes. Everything's fine." Her voice tightened, as did her hold on the mug.

Please, Lord! Make him back off! I don't want to talk about this.

Unfortunately, God didn't seem to be tuned in to her frequency today.

"Listen…I don't want to pry, Kelsey, but we're neighbors. Temporarily, anyway. And I know you're alone. Hannah told me you're not married, and that the baby's father is out of the picture." He lifted his hand to his glasses. Hesitated. Then took them off.

All at once she found herself drowning in warm, brown eyes that were awash with empathy and caring.

"So I wanted to tell you that if you need anything while I'm here, don't hesitate to ask."

Pressure built in her throat, behind her eyes, and she gritted her teeth. She was not going to cry! She was not going to fall apart just because a nice man had made a kind offer.

But much to her dismay, a tear managed to leak out and trickle down her cheek.

Before she could swipe it away, Luke reached over and did it for her with a lean finger, his tender touch melting her heart.

"What's wrong, Kelsey? Can you tell me?"

Choking back a sob, she shook her head and stood, the uneven sand only partly to blame for her unsteadiness. Without bothering to fold up her chair, she stumbled toward the path in the tall grass.

"Kelsey! Wait!"

She ignored Luke's call and plunged into the grass, praying he wouldn't follow.

At the landing halfway up, she risked a glance back toward the beach while she caught her breath. Luke was standing by his chair, the morning sun bronzing his face as he looked up toward her. His tall, stalwart form reminded her of the prince heroes who'd peopled the fairy tales she'd devoured as a child.

But she'd given those stories up years ago, much preferring to take care of herself rather than rely on a man. She liked being strong. In control of her life. Successful in her own right.

Besides, knights on white horses were in short supply in today's world.

And happy endings were even more rare, as divorce statistics proved.

She turned away from Luke and continued up the steps—a trek that was becoming more difficult with each passing day. But she could deal with it. Or any other challenge that came her way.

Yet, for one fleeting moment, she wondered what it would be like to have a man like Luke by her side. Not to hold her up, but to hold her hand.

In the next instant, she ruthlessly quashed that thought.

For given her situation, it, too, was the stuff of fairy tales.

As Kelsey disappeared from view, Luke raked his fingers through his hair.

Talk about a bust.

Expelling a frustrated breath, he sank back into his beach chair, closed his eyes and folded his hands on his stomach. So much for following Hannah's advice about letting Kelsey know he was interested in her life. He'd tried to open the door to some confidences, but she'd slammed it in his face. And bolted as fast as a startled deer.

Now he was back to square one. He wouldn't be surprised if the next time they met, every bit of the wariness she'd exhibited at their first encounter would be back in place.

The prospect left a hollow feeling in the pit of his stomach.

"You blew it, didn't you?"

At Hannah's comment, Luke stifled a groan and opened his eyes. She stood beside him, hands on hips, shaking her head in disgust.

"I set you up perfectly. All you had to do was ask a few discreet, caring questions about the baby." She crossed her arms. "So what did you say, anyway? I saw her take off like a bat out of…you know where. It must have been bad."

"Since when did you become Dr. Phil?"

She wrinkled her brow. "Who?"

Wrong demographic. Kids her age probably had their own relationship guru. He waved her into her seat. "Let it go, Hannah. I don't need advice about my love life."

"Ah-ha! You admit you're falling in love. Now we're getting somewhere." She dropped down onto the side of her chair, putting them at eye level.

"I'm not admitting anything." He shot her a disgruntled look.

"Fine. Whatever. So what did you say to her?" She leaned toward him, posture intent.

Luke shifted in his chair. He had a feeling she wasn't going to like his response. But it was also clear she wasn't going to let him off the hook. He'd have to throw her a few crumbs.

"I followed your advice about letting her know I cared. I told her I knew she wasn't married, and that if she needed anything while I was here, all she had to do was ask."

In the silence that followed, Hannah squinted at him. "That's it?"

He replayed the conversation in his mind. "I also told her she looked tired, and I asked if everything was okay."

She waited, as if she expected him to continue. When he didn't, she shook her head and flopped back in her chair. As if he were a hopeless case.

"Did you tell her anything about yourself, Luke?"

"Like what?"

"Like anything that would give her a glimpse into who you are. Into what makes you tick."

"You didn't mention that yesterday."

"I didn't think I had to. It's Relationships 101. If you don't share with another person and show you trust them with your secrets, how do you expect them to trust you with theirs?"

Okay. She had a point. But being tutored on romance by a seventeen-year-old was bruising his ego. Time to go on the defensive.

"You know, I've gotten along fine without your advice for the twenty-plus years I've been dating. I've never had any trouble relating to the women I went out with."

"Yeah? Then how come you're still single?"

Checkmate.

He grasped at the excuse he'd always given. "I was too busy for romance in medical school. And my army career didn't lend itself to commitments."

"The right woman would have changed your mind about that. If you'd ever let anyone get close enough to see into your heart. You can't fall in love or develop a real friendship if you keep all your emotions locked up tight."

A muscle clenched in Luke's jaw, and he averted his head to stare out over the water, now sparkling in the morning sun as if sprinkled by diamonds.

"Maybe not. But it's the only way to survive when you witness death and destruction every day. When you deal with young men and women whose lives are snuffed out or forever changed in an instant by a bullet or by fire from an explosion or by a roadside bomb. You learn not to feel too deeply. Not to invest too much of yourself. Because if you let yourself feel too much, you die, too. Little by little, day by day, until the heart that once beat with passion is an empty shell. So you lock it up to protect it. And it's hard to unlock once it's been sealed." His voice hoarsened, and he closed his eyes, fighting for control.

After a few seconds, he felt a gentle touch on his arm.

Blinking away the moisture that clouded his vision, he swallowed. "Sorry."

"Don't be." Her tone was soft. Sympathetic. And when he turned his head toward her, her eyes were moist as well. "That's what I'm talking about, Luke. What you just did. It's okay to share that with people you care about. It's what helps them feel close to you. And love you. Could you use a hug, maybe?"

Once more his throat tightened. Without speaking, he rose and held out his arms. Hannah stepped in, and he folded her close.

As he clung to her in the quiet morning, the silence broken only by the lap of waves on the shore and the rustle of the tall grass behind the beach, swaying in the wind, he let out a long, unsteady breath. It had been years since anyone had comforted him like this. And it felt good.

"From the time you came home on your first leave when I was eight, looking all impressive in your uniform, you were my hero." Hannah's voice was muffled against his chest. "You still are."

He shook his head. "I'm no hero, Hannah."

"Then why did the army give you the Silver Star, among other medals?"

"I just did what I had to do."

"With honor and courage. And that makes you a hero in my book. Not to mention what you're doing for Carlos." She pulled back and searched his face. "Do you remember how in awe of you I was on that first leave?"

A smile tugged at one corner of his mouth as he pictured the little blonde pixie who'd followed him everywhere. "I remember I couldn't shake you."

She made a face and nudged him with her shoulder. "I hung on your every word. And I was desperate to impress you. To show you I was courageous, too. That's why I climbed the apple tree out back. Instead, I fell on my face and got a bloody nose. Do you remember that?"

The image of Hannah's tear-streaked cheeks niggled at the edge of his memory. "Vaguely."

"It's a vivid memory for me. And what you said stuck with me all these years, too. After you extracted a promise from me never to climb that tree again, you sat me on your knee and said, 'Being brave isn't about doing a dangerous thing, Hannah. It's about doing the right thing. Even when it's hard.'"

"I said that?"

"Yeah. I guess it was one of your rare profound moments." She smirked at him, then grew more serious. "But it was good advice, Luke. And maybe it applies to Kelsey."

The conversation had come full circle.

"I'm not sure what the right thing is with her."

"That, dear brother, is where prayer comes in. Ask God." With one final squeeze, she extricated herself from his arms and folded up her chair. "You ready to call it a morning? I told Dorothy I'd be there by noon today to help with the lunch rush."

"Yeah." He picked up his own chair as well as Kelsey's and tucked them under one arm. Then he retrieved his coffee and his neighbor's lidded, insulated mug. The white residue around the lip suggested it contained milk.

As he trudged through the tall grass behind Hannah and started up the steps, her advice replayed in his mind. *Ask God.* It was the same advice Carlos had always dispensed. Except the young medic had used more colloquial language: *when in doubt, give God a shout.* And it had always been delivered with a grin.

Well, Luke had plenty of doubts when it came to Kelsey. Should he try again to connect? Make the first move toward sharing confidences? Take the risk of getting involved, knowing he was leaving in four short weeks?

At the top of the steps, he stopped and glanced toward her cottage. It showed no signs of life. But she was inside. No way could she have gotten ready for work and left already.

"Hannah, I'm going to drop Kelsey's stuff off at her house."

His sister acknowledged his comment with a wave and kept moving toward their deck.

Detouring toward his neighbor's, Luke circled

around the small cluster of trees rather than cutting through them. If she was outside, by chance, he didn't want to startle her. Been there, done that.

But the yard and screened porch were deserted. Leaning the chair against the railing beside the two steps, he opened the porch door and set the mug inside. Away from the bugs.

As he turned to leave, he thought he detected a flutter in the curtains at one of the back windows. Was she watching him? Hoping he'd knock—or praying he'd leave? In their short acquaintance, he'd seen both loneliness and fear in her eyes. Which dominated at the moment?

Instead of waiting to find out, Luke retraced his steps across the lawn. Kelsey needed to be receptive to a second overture, or it would fail as dismally as his clumsy earlier effort had. And his instincts told him today wasn't the day to try again.

Nor was he up for the kind of soul-baring Hannah seemed to think it would take to earn Kelsey's trust. Not yet. He'd have to work himself into that mind-set.

But he didn't have a lot of time. The clock was ticking on his stay here.

After ascending the steps to his deck, Luke paused at the railing to look once more at the horizon, where sky and sea met. And to follow the advice Hannah and Carlos agreed upon.

If you want me to get involved here, Lord, please give me an opportunity to win Kelsey's trust. And if You do that, please also give me the courage to be the hero Hannah thinks I am.

Chapter Ten

"Tea break!"

At Dorothy's announcement, Kelsey looked up from the quilt rack where she was trying to make some headway on a commission due at the end of August—a short three weeks away.

"You sound especially cheery today. Let's see..." Kelsey leaned back in her chair and regarded her friends. "Your upbeat mood wouldn't have anything to do with a certain gentleman who's been enjoying quite a few solitary lunches in the tearoom, would it?"

Bright pink spots appeared on Dorothy's cheeks as she deposited a cup of tea and a plate of scones on a small table next to the quilt rack. "I didn't think you'd noticed."

"I didn't. Hannah tipped me off. She calls him your beau."

The woman's flush deepened. "I'm too old to have a beau. Besides, he's younger than me."

Kelsey raised an eyebrow. Hannah had pointed out the dapper, white-haired man to her yesterday. "How much younger?"

"He's only seventy-one."

Kelsey adopted a look of mock horror. "Goodness! You'd be robbing the cradle!" She picked up a scone and nibbled at it. "When was I going to hear about this new development, anyway? I tell you everything."

"I was going to mention it eventually. If it lasted. We only met two weeks ago. I thought his interest might wane."

"According to Hannah, he comes for lunch almost every day. I don't think his interest is waning." She inspected the scone in her hand. "This is delicious, by the way. I don't recall you ever making chocolate chip scones before. New recipe?"

Dorothy's color surged again. "Charles likes chocolate."

"Ah. That explains it. So tell me all about this mystery man." Kelsey grinned at her and continued to eat. She couldn't ever recall seeing the older woman flustered. Then again, love—or even mere attraction—could do that to a person.

She was finding that out firsthand.

"His name is Charles Summer. He and his wife used to rent a condo in Holland every August after he retired, but this is the first time he's come back since she died three years ago. He doesn't get into Douglas much, but over the Fourth of July weekend he joined some old friends from out of town for lunch at the tearoom. We chatted a little that day, and he started coming back. More conversations led to a dinner invitation…and we've been seeing each other ever since."

Finishing off her scone, Kelsey picked up her teacup. "That's a very romantic story, Dorothy."

"I'm too old for romance."

"No one's ever too old for romance."

"We'll see, I suppose." The older woman smoothed back a stray strand of hair. "And speaking of romance, I haven't seen Luke much lately."

Kelsey shot Dorothy a cautious look. "What does Luke have to do with romance?"

"You tell me. Hannah thinks there are sparks between the two of you."

"Hannah has a very active imagination. I've hardly seen Luke in the past two weeks. Now that the campaign is beginning to attract national media attention, he's been on the go every minute."

"I think there are sparks, too."

"Then you have an overactive imagination as well."

"Hmm." Dorothy fingered her pearls. "You never did tell me what Dr. Walters had to say about this new man in your life."

This was not a discussion Kelsey wanted to have.

She set down her teacup, bent her head over the quilt and went back to work. "He's not the new man in my life, Dorothy. Not in the way you mean. But he is nice, and I do find him attractive. Dr. Walters thinks that's a positive sign. I agree. Meeting him has been very therapeutic."

"Therapeutic." The older woman burst into laughter. "I wonder what your neighbor would say if he heard you describing him that way?"

Kelsey shot her an appalled look, but Dorothy waved her concerns aside.

"Don't worry, my dear. Your secret is safe with me."

With that, she retreated to her own side of the shop.

Leaving Kelsey to wonder what secret she'd been referring to—the secret about her baby, or the secret about her growing feelings for the doctor next door.

Hannah touched her white linen napkin to her lips and gave a satisfied sigh. "That was an amazing meal, Luke. Thanks for the great send-off."

"I'm glad you enjoyed it." He signaled the waiter for a refill of his coffee. "More tea, Kelsey?"

"No, thanks. I've reached my limit. And I second Hannah's comment about the food. I haven't been here in years, but Clearbrook was always a wonderful special occasion place. The food is just as good as I remember." She smoothed her fingers over the starched tablecloth. "Gram and Dorothy were born three weeks apart, and they used to come here to celebrate their birthdays every year. Too bad Dorothy couldn't join us tonight."

"She offered to back out on her date with Charles, but he had tickets for a play in Grand Rapids she's dying to see, so I told her to go for it. We said our good-byes this afternoon. I wouldn't want to stand in the way of romance." Aiming a deliberate look at her brother, Hannah picked up her purse. "Would you two excuse me while I run to the ladies' room?"

Luke resisted the urge to roll his eyes at her obvious strategy. Kelsey had gone to the rest room ten minutes ago, and Hannah had declined to join her. Apparently she'd been planning all along to give them a few minutes alone in this romantic, candlelit spot.

Not that it would do much good. Kelsey was chasing some crumbs from her molten chocolate cake around her plate with her fork—and avoiding his eyes. Just as she'd been avoiding him on the beach for the past ten days. When their paths did cross on the afternoons he picked up Hannah from the tearoom, she used the occasion to get updates on the youth center project and fill him in on her latest PR efforts.

As far as he was concerned, if God wanted this relationship to deepen, He wasn't offering Luke much opportunity to take it to the next level.

Eyeing Kelsey, he picked up his coffee. "I want to thank you for taking Hannah under your wing during her visit."

"I enjoyed getting to know her." Kelsey set her fork on her plate and looked at him. "She was a godsend to Dorothy, too. Losing a server had her in a tizzy until Hannah stepped forward and volunteered to fill in while she rounded up a replacement."

"Things worked out well all around. Much better than I expected after her first day on the beach."

A smile tugged at the corners of Kelsey's lips and she lifted her teacup. "You did seem a little panicked when she was flirting with those two college guys."

"Guilty as charged." He raised his cup in acknowledgement. "But much to my relief, she told me later that since she was only going to be here for three weeks, there was no sense starting something that would go nowhere."

Kelsey rested her elbows on the table, cradling the teacup in her hands as she met his gaze. "She has a point."

"I agree. Especially at that age." He edged the conversation onto personal ground, choosing his next words with care. "But friendships don't have to be bound by geography. If people are willing to make the effort."

He held his breath as she studied him. He expected her to shut down. Or divert the conversation to a safer topic. But she surprised him.

Setting her cup in its saucer, she clasped her hands together and rested them on the edge of the table. "Luke...I haven't missed Hannah's less-than-subtle efforts to push us together. Dorothy's been dropping hints, too. But you'll be gone in three weeks. We hardly know each other. And relationships among mature adults come with a lot of baggage that can be very difficult to deal with in person, let alone over a long distance."

Kelsey's candor took him off guard. As did the melancholy sadness deep in her eyes. But if she was cracking the door, he was stepping through. With both feet.

"Are you talking about the baby?"

She rested a hand on her stomach. Swallowed. Opened her mouth to respond.

"Will there be anything else, sir?" The waiter stopped beside him and slid the check onto the table.

Kelsey closed her mouth and reached for her purse.

The moment was gone.

Stifling his disappointment, he pulled his credit card out of his wallet and handed it over. "No. Thanks."

As the waiter walked away, Hannah rejoined them. "Did I miss anything important?" She sent him a hopeful look.

"No."

Her face fell.

"What time is your flight tomorrow, Hannah?" Kelsey's question redirected the conversation to more mundane matters, where it remained during the short ride home in the dark.

When they parted in the driveway, Kelsey hugged Hannah, murmured her thanks to Luke for dinner, and disappeared around the trees with an "I'll be fine," after he offered to walk her to her door.

The instant the darkness swallowed her, Hannah turned to him. "So why didn't you use the ambiance at the restaurant to your advantage while I was gone? Draw her out a little?"

"I tried. But the waiter interrupted us."

"That figures." Hannah blew out a frustrated breath. "Well, you're on your own after I leave, big brother. Work on it, okay?"

"I'll pray about it. That's the best I can promise." He opened the door and moved aside to allow her to precede him.

"Good plan. I'll add my voice. Wherever two or three and all that." She stopped in the living room to give him a hug. "I need to finish packing. See you tomorrow."

"Sleep well."

She disappeared down the hall, and Luke wandered into the kitchen. Opening the back door, he stepped out and strolled across the deck. The moon was slivering the whitecaps on the lake, and stars twinkled above. He couldn't imagine a more peaceful scene.

Yet as he glanced next door through the darkness, he had a feeling the tranquility of the setting would be lost on his neighbor. Despite her faith, despite a career she appeared to enjoy, despite her apparent peace with her decision to leave the corporate world, she seemed weighed down with worry. And a sadness that was soul deep.

Tonight, for the first time, she'd admitted she carried baggage. Not only that, he was certain she'd been on the cusp of giving him a glimpse into the secrets locked in her heart—until the waiter interrupted them.

But if she'd come that close once, perhaps she would again. Given the right circumstances.

And he intended to do everything in his power to *create* those circumstances, if necessary, before he headed south to start his E.R. director job in Atlanta.

Kelsey couldn't remember ever being so tired.

As she massaged the small of her back, she halfheartedly pulled a frying pan from the cabinet and tried to work up some enthusiasm for the evening meal. But no way could a sautéed chicken breast and simple salad compete with last night's dinner at Clearbrook. The oyster-and-asparagus chowder had been to die for, and the pan-seared New Zealand lamb had melted in her mouth.

Not that it mattered. She wasn't hungry tonight anyway. Plus, she had a nagging backache. Too many hours on her feet at the shop, no doubt. But sitting at the quilt rack had proven uncomfortable, too—even though she needed to make some significant progress on her commission soon.

She pulled out a can of vegetable spray and coated the pan. Maybe if she put her feet up and—

A knock sounded behind her, and her hand jerked, sending a swath of glistening oil across the stovetop.

Only two people had ever come to the back of her house. And one of them had flown home to Atlanta today.

Meaning her visitor was Luke.

She set the can of vegetable spray on the counter, wiped her palms on her skirt and tried to downshift her pulse. *Please, Lord, don't let him try to pick up last night's interrupted dinner conversation! Hannah was right. There's no sense starting something that has no future. I should never have let the intimate ambiance at the restaurant prod me into beginning a discussion I don't want to finish.*

Another knock sounded. This one louder than the first.

The temptation to ignore the summons was strong. But that would be childish. He knew she was here. Her car was in the drive and lights were on all over the house.

Psyching herself up for the encounter, she moved to the back door, summoned up a smile and exited into the screened porch. He was standing outside the porch, dressed in a chest-hugging T-shirt and worn jeans that sat well on his lean hips, and despite her efforts to rein it in, her pulse shifted into high gear again as she approached him.

"Hi. Did Hannah get off okay?" She almost pulled off her attempt at a bright, friendly— impersonal—tone.

"Yes. I heard from her a little while ago. She's home safe and sound. Am I interrupting anything?" He motioned toward her left hand.

She looked down. Her fingers were dusted with flour, and she swiped them on her skirt, leaving white streaks on the denim. "No. I was just fixing dinner. Nothing to rival last night. Thank you again for including me."

"It was my pleasure. May I come in for a minute? I borrowed this from Father Joe after today's board meeting and I thought you'd be interested in seeing it." He held up a large black portfolio case. "Once we got a gentleman's agreement on the land purchase, the architectural firm started working on some preliminary drawings for the youth center. We wanted to have some concrete ideas to show at the fundraising dinner."

He was here on business. Good. Business she could handle.

Pushing open the door, she stepped aside to let him enter. "Is that large enough?" She gestured toward the café table in the center of the room.

"Should be."

He walked over to it, unzipped the case and pulled out three color artist's renderings. "They're very different styles. Take a look and tell me which one you like best."

Curious, she joined him at the table and leaned over to examine the drawings. All three were appealing, but one caught her eye immediately. It was a low-slung structure, constructed of glass, wood and stone, and the irregular shape lent itself to interesting rooflines that peaked and soared in several places.

"No contest. That one." She pointed to it. "It's stunning."

"That was my choice, too. We must have similar tastes."

At his husky comment, she looked over her shoulder. Only to discover he was mere inches away.

Her heart stuttered, then raced on, as she got lost in his dark brown eyes. Funny. She'd never noticed the flecks of gold in them before. Or the thin white scar near his hairline. As for the sensuous curve of his firm lips…

Dr. Walters had advised that she let herself experience attraction in a safe environment. But standing ten inches from Luke Turner suddenly didn't feel in the least bit safe.

As she gripped the back of the chair in front of her and tried to regain her equilibrium, the phone began to ring.

Thank You, Lord!

The spell broken, she eased away from Luke and backed toward the door. "I need to get that. Thanks for bringing those over." She motioned toward the table.

"No problem." He picked up her favorite. "After you finish your call, I'll give you the highlights of the architect's comments on this one."

He wasn't leaving.

Behind her, she groped for the doorknob, twisting it as she fought down a rush of panic. "This could take a while. And I haven't eaten dinner yet."

He sat on the wicker settee, his actions deliberate, his gaze steady. "I'm in no hurry. I don't have any plans for tonight. But I promise not to delay your dinner long."

Pushing through the door, she fled. Certain now that Luke had more he wanted to discuss than the architect's comments.

Focused on developing an evasion strategy, Kelsey picked up the phone and gave the caller a distracted greeting.

"Ms. Anderson?"

The male voice was familiar, but she couldn't place it. "Yes."

"This is Detective Mark Layton from St. Louis County Crimes Against Persons. Do you have a few minutes?"

A shock wave ricocheted through her, and she sucked in a sharp breath. An image of the detective's face clicked into place—along with all the other details of that terrible night. Feeling for the stool beside her, she lowered herself to it as the stiffening went out of her legs.

"Ms. Anderson?"

"Yes." The word came out strained and barely audible.

"I wanted to let you know we have a suspect in custody. His last victim managed to inflict some damage to his face that raised red flags when he was stopped two days later for a traffic violation. We're running DNA now, but the details of the latest crime fit his MO. I think we have our man. I'll keep you informed, but I thought you'd want to know."

"Wh-who is it?"

"A guy named Carl Williams. A real loser. Caucasian, twenty-nine, a history of minor run-ins with the law. Does the name ring any bells?"

"No."

"I didn't think it would. But I'd like to email you his photo. Just in case you recognize him."

As he recited the email address she'd given him seven months ago, she began to shake.

They wanted her to look at his face.

She closed her eyes and forced herself to take a deep breath.

You can do this, Kelsey.

"Is that still correct, Ms. Anderson?"

"Yes." A tremor ran through her voice. "I'll check my email later tonight, if that's all right."

"That's fine."

"Do I...have to do anything else?"

"Not at this point. None of the victims can ID him, but the DNA should be all the evidence we need. If this goes to trial, you may be called on to testify, but that will be months down the road."

Kelsey tightened her grip on the phone. She couldn't even imagine recounting her story and reliving the nightmare in front of a roomful of people. Yet she wanted the man punished. To the full extent of the law. If that took a court appearance, she'd find the strength to do it.

But what had he meant by "if"?

"Is there a chance this might not go to trial?"

"It's possible. He could plea-bargain. Plead guilty in exchange for leniency in sentencing. Frankly, I hope he doesn't. We'd like to stick it to this guy. He doesn't deserve one iota of consideration."

The hard edge to the detective's voice reflected her own feelings.

"I hope he doesn't, either. Thank you for letting me know. I'll get back to you later tonight."

"Good enough. Take care."

The line went dead.

As the seconds ticked by, Kelsey sat there, phone still pressed to her ear, staring at the far wall.

She couldn't think. Couldn't move. Couldn't handle the flood of emotions the call had unleashed.

All along, she thought she'd dealt with the attack. After a lot of prayer, after hours of conversation with Dr. Walters and Reverend Howard, she'd come to accept that, while she'd made a mistake, she wasn't to blame for what had happened. God hadn't been punishing her. She was the victim.

And she hadn't let it destroy her. Instead, she'd used it as a wake-up call to build a different, better life. Residual fear and wariness were understandable. But they were dissipating now, too. Thanks in large part to a kind, caring army doctor who even now sat waiting for her just steps away.

A man who was fast making inroads into her heart.

A man she'd be interested in getting to know better if her life wasn't so complicated.

As if on cue, one of those complications gave her a kick.

Resting her hand atop the new, innocent life within her, Kelsey's throat tightened. She couldn't let herself get involved with Luke until she made some decisions about this baby. That was only fair to him.

But hours of thinking and multiple prayers hadn't yet yielded any guidance.

And Luke was leaving in seventeen days.

A raucous beep began to sound in her ear, reminding her the phone was off the hook. She fumbled it back into the holder and tried to blink away the moisture blurring her vision. But a tear escaped out of the corner of her eye and trailed down her check. Followed by another. And another. Until there were more than she could control.

And she hated being out of control.

Dr. Walters had warned her tears would come at some point. *Should* come. That crying was more than okay. It was cathartic. But this wasn't the time. Not with Luke waiting for her.

Resting her elbows on the counter, she buried her face in her hands.

Don't panic, Kelsey. Just breathe. You'll be fine.

That mantra had always worked in the past, and she repeated it over and over. Waiting for calm to replace panic. Waiting for her respiration to steady. Waiting for her pulse to slow.

But as the tears continued to course down her cheeks, her heart wasn't listening.

Luke tapped the foam-backed rendering in his hand with one finger and frowned. Kelsey had said she might be a while, but fifteen minutes seemed excessive. Maybe she hoped he'd get tired of waiting and leave.

No way. He wasn't going to let her off as easily this time. Tonight, he was going to get answers to at least some of his questions.

Rising from the wicker settee, he put the rendering back on the table and moved to the door. She'd shut it behind her, but through the window he had a partial side view of her. She was seated at the counter with her back to him, and the phone had been returned to its holder. The call was over.

But the effects weren't. Her face was buried in her hands and her shoulders were shaking.

She was crying.

Jolted, he stared at her. His next-door neighbor didn't strike him as the type of woman who cried without serious provocation.

Something bad had happened.

He reached for the door, following his first impulse. Kelsey needed comforting, and his instincts told him to pull her into a hug as Hannah had done with him not long ago.

But Kelsey had always kept him at arm's length. Such a move could backfire.

He went to plan B.

Instead of opening the door, he lifted his hand and rapped lightly on the glass. "Kelsey?"

His query carried through the open window farther down the wall, and her body went rigid. She raised her head, but kept it averted as she gripped the edge of the counter.

"Another time would be better, Luke."

He hardly recognized her strained, shaky voice.

Without waiting for him to respond, she edged sideways down the length of the counter, her back to him. She paused for a moment to grasp the back of a kitchen chair, as if to steady herself, then headed toward the hall.

"Kelsey, wait!"

At his entreaty, she picked up her pace.

Not a good move in her condition.

Two steps later, when she cut the hall corner too short and bumped into the wall, she stumbled. Teetered. Flailed for a handhold.

Adrenaline surging, Luke yanked open the back door, sprinted across the room and grabbed for her as she went down. He was in time to keep her from falling flat. But not in time to prevent her from going down hard on one knee.

Crouching beside her, he kept a firm grip on her arm. She was bent over, one hand on the floor, the other on her stomach. Her soft, blond hair had swung forward, hiding her face from his view, but he could hear her ragged gasps.

He could also feel her shaking.

"It's okay, Kelsey." He used his most soothing voice as he stroked her back. "You'll be fine. Let me help you to a chair." Without waiting for a response, he rose, bent toward her and extended his hand. After a moment she took it. "On three. One, two, three."

Her grip tightened as he helped her to her feet. And he didn't let go once she was upright. Because as soon as she tried to put weight on her injured knee, she winced.

"Let's get you off your feet." He put his arm around her waist and, absorbing as much of her weight as he could, he led her to a kitchen chair and eased her into it. Then he dropped down to balance on the balls of his feet beside her, planning to examine her knee.

"I'm more worried…about the baby."

At her tremulous comment, he lifted his head—and got his first gut-clenching glimpse of her ravaged face. Her eyes were red and puffy, her cheeks moist with tears, her lips taut and trembling. She looked as traumatized as some of the patients he'd treated on the battlefield.

Struggling to disguise his shock, he did his best to reassure her about the baby. "I don't think the fall was hard enough to cause any problems on that score."

He forced himself to focus on her knee, which was tender to the touch and already showing signs of discoloration. But a quick exam relieved his mind.

"I don't think there's any serious damage, but it may swell, and it will definitely bruise. Do you have an ice pack in the house?"

"Gram had one. It's in the hall closet." She waved toward the narrow passage where she'd been heading when she'd fallen.

Her voice was still shaky. Too shaky.

"I'll get it, then we'll move you somewhere more comfortable so you can elevate your leg."

He strode down the hall toward the closet at the end, glancing into each of the three rooms he passed. One contained quilt paraphernalia. The other two were bedrooms.

There was no sign of a nursery. Nor any indication a room was being readied to house the infant being carried by the traumatized woman in the kitchen.

As he opened the closet door and searched the shelves for the ice pack, he reached a decision.

He wasn't leaving this house until he had answers to *all* the questions that had left him tossing in bed for the past dozen nights.

And if he had to open his own heart and go way outside his comfort zone to get them, so be it.

Chapter Eleven

As Kelsey waited for Luke to return, she rested her hand on her stomach and felt for signs of life. Despite his reassurance about the baby, the fall had been jarring. And she'd come too far on this journey not to see it through.

A powerful kick widened her eyes—and set her mind at ease. It was almost as if the baby was saying, "Hey, knock off the rough stuff." But as long as her child was okay, he or she could kick up a storm.

The sound of a door closing down the hall redirected her thoughts. Time to switch gears and figure out how to deal with Luke. After witnessing her meltdown, he wasn't likely to walk out without asking questions she wasn't ready to answer. Too bad she hadn't been alone when the call came in from Detective Layton.

"Everything okay?" He paused on his way to the refrigerator for ice, and gave her an assessing scan.

"Yes. Thanks. Look, you don't have to hang around. I can take care of my knee."

He ignored her comment. "Give me a minute and I'll help you to the couch so you can put your foot up."

Message: You're not getting rid of me.

She watched the muscles flex in his broad back as he opened the refrigerator, and her vision once more blurred. She wasn't used to having anyone wait on her here. Not since Gram had died. Dorothy fed her scones and tea and fussed over her at the shop, but at the cottage she'd been on her own.

Until now.

And it felt good to have someone take care of her.

Her eyes brimmed, and she brushed away the moisture with the back of her hand. Breaking down in front of this man was not an option. If she ever decided to tell him about her past, it would be on her own terms. At a time and place of her choosing. And it would be a controlled, clinical retelling. No emotions. Just the facts, in a neutral location with bright sunlight.

The cozy haven of Gram's cottage, burnished with the intimate, golden glow of the setting sun, was not that setting.

So she'd let him help her over to the couch. Feign tiredness. And hope he got the hint that she wanted him to leave.

Rejoining her, he set the ice pack on the table

and held out his hand. "Okay. Let's get you on your feet."

In silence, she placed her hand in his. His lean fingers closed over hers and he pulled her to her feet in one smooth, effortless motion that bunched the impressive muscles below the sleeve of his T-shirt.

A little trill ran along her nerve endings, and she averted her head, irritated. She needed to stick with her plan, not be swayed by hormones that were way out of control at this stage of her pregnancy.

Once she was on her feet, he moved beside her and put his arm around her waist. What there was of it.

"Just lean on me."

The soft, husky words loosened her tear ducts again.

Hang on, Kelsey! Just get to the couch. Once you're settled, you can send him on his way.

As they traversed the small living room, she found herself leaning on him a lot more than she'd planned. Her knee was throbbing, and she could feel the skin stretching as it swelled. A tear spilled out of the corner of her eye, and she tried to surreptitiously wipe it away after he eased her onto the soft cushions.

"I'll be right back."

He disappeared down the hall. She had no idea where he was going, but the reprieve gave her a chance to regain control.

When he reappeared sixty seconds later, she had

herself together. More or less. But he'd been busy, too. Two pillows were tucked under one arm, a lap quilt was draped over the other, and he was holding a box of tissues in one hand and a bottle of Tylenol in the other. He set the quilt by her feet, handed her the tissues and gave the bottle a little shake.

"Is your OB okay with these? They're generally safe during pregnancy."

"Yes. She said they were fine, in moderation."

"Good. They'll help with the discomfort in your knee." He set the bottle on the arm of the couch and offered a hand. "Grab hold and I'll pull you up so I can put these pillows behind you."

She did as he instructed, trying to ignore the broad, muscular shoulder that brushed hers as he arranged the pillows.

"Okay." He lowered her gently back, set the ice pack on her knee and draped the quilt over her. "I saw a chicken breast on the counter in the kitchen. Was that supposed to be your dinner?"

She bobbed her head, not trusting her voice.

"I'm not much into cooking, but if you have some eggs, I can handle an omelet."

He wanted to cook her dinner.

The faucet behind her eyes began to drip again.

"Y-you don't have to do that. Besides, I'm not hungry anymore." She'd wanted the comment to sound firm. Instead, the words came out ragged and tear-laced.

"There are a lot of things I don't have to do,

Kelsey. But sometimes you do things because they're the right thing to do." His serious gaze held hers for a few seconds, then he lightened his tone. "Do you have eggs and cheese?"

"Yes."

"How about mushrooms?"

"Yes."

"Perfect. Give me five minutes."

From her propped-up sitting position, she watched him through the pass-through that divided the kitchen from the living room. He worked methodically, with a natural efficiency of motion that came as no surprise. Luke struck her as the kind of man who made every moment count, no matter the task.

While her dinner cooked, he brought a kitchen chair in and set it beside her. Not a good sign. He must be planning to stay while she ate. And how could she tell him to get lost after all he'd done to help her tonight?

When he returned with a fluffy, golden-brown omelet, a glass of milk and some Tylenol tablets, he surprised her by setting the items on the chair beside her.

So he wasn't planning to sit there after all.

A surge of disappointment took her off guard, and she scrunched the quilt in her fists, doing her best to squelch the unwelcome emotion. She should be glad he was leaving. It was what she'd wanted.

"Do you need anything else?"

She swallowed past the tightness in her throat and

shook her head. "No. Thank you. Sorry to put you to all this trouble."

"It was no trouble, Kelsey."

He moved to the end of the small sofa, and before she realized his intent he lifted her legs, edged under them, and sat. After lowering them to his lap, he readjusted the ice pack and rested his hands lightly on her quilt-covered legs.

"Go ahead and eat your omelet before it gets cold." He gestured to the food on the chair beside her. "Then we'll talk."

Kelsey stared at him. He expected her to eat while he held her legs? And with the specter of a serious discussion looming?

No way would she be able to choke down even one bite.

When she made no move to pick up the plate, he leaned over and retrieved it for her. "Come on. Try a few bites. You don't want to insult the cook."

He smiled at her, his eyes warm and coaxing, his features relaxed and reassuring, as if to say, "You have nothing to fear from me, Kelsey. I'm on your side. You're safe."

And truth be told, she did feel safe. And protected. And cared for. More than she had for a very long time. More than she had even prior to that fateful December night.

Maybe it was an illusion. Maybe once Luke heard her story he'd disappear. But for this moment, she decided to take the comfort he was willing to offer.

To pretend she wasn't in this all by herself. To let go of the fear and uncertainty and loneliness, if only for a few minutes.

Lifting her fork, she took a bite of the tender omelet. It was bursting with cheese and mushrooms, and subtly infused with a tang she couldn't identify.

"This is very good." She cut off a second bite. "I'm picking up some unusual flavors."

He grinned. "I raided your spice cabinet. Onion flakes, a dash of tarragon and a few flakes of oregano. My mom makes great omelets, and she loves to experiment. Most of her concoctions succeed, but none of us have ever let her live down the salmon, blue cheese and capers omelet she made a few years ago when I came home on leave."

"Bad?"

"Awful. Hannah said it stunk, and declared she couldn't eat anything that smelled that bad. Mom cajoled her into taking one bite, after which she promptly threw up. All over the table. While she crawled off to bed, Dad and I went to IHOP."

A laugh bubbled up inside Kelsey, and she took another bite, realizing she was wolfing down the simple meal. And wishing she had more. "Your effort is much more palatable."

"Thanks. I've learned that a little risk-taking pays off with omelets. And with life. You just have to be careful not to push the limits so far you end up with a disaster on your hands."

One glance at his serious demeanor confirmed he wasn't talking about omelets anymore.

The final bite stuck in her throat, and she picked up her glass of milk to wash it down.

"We need to talk, Kelsey."

She swallowed and gripped her glass. All at once, the fluffy omelet felt heavy in her stomach, and she had an inkling of Hannah's reaction to his mother's bizarre concoction.

"I'll start."

At his unexpected comment, she lifted her chin and gave him a wary look.

A few beats of silence passed—as if he were gathering his thoughts…or his courage. Kelsey's nervousness gave way to curiosity, and her pulse steadied.

"You know I came to Michigan to launch the youth center project." His resonant baritone voice and calm tone soothed her. "But I also wanted some downtime and solitude after ten years in a pressure-cooker environment. I wanted to lie on a private beach and let the world go by without having to worry about watching my back every minute, or losing sleep over the lives I hadn't been able to save that day."

He stroked her leg through the quilt as he spoke, but his attention was on a wall hanging Gram had made, which had occupied the place of honor on the far wall for more than two decades. The sunburst motif featured the three words that had guided Bess Anderson's life: "Live. Love. Rejoice."

"Things didn't work out quite the way I'd hoped, though. First, I discovered I didn't have a private beach. Then Hannah needed a place to stay. The youth center project also took off—thanks to your publicity efforts—and I didn't have a spare minute in the day. Finally, most unsettling of all, I found myself worrying about my new neighbor."

He turned his head toward her, and at his tender expression, her heart melted.

"I didn't want to worry about you, Kelsey. I fought it every step of the way. Yet the more we worked together, the more you intrigued—and attracted— me. Sparks began to fly. I wanted to know more about you, but you kept me at arm's length. I've learned to recognize fear over these past ten years, and I saw it in you from the beginning. I don't know why you're afraid, but I do understand fear. And I know firsthand how it can paralyze a person— in a lot of different ways."

He clasped his hands together, the muscles in his throat working as he focused on his fingers.

"Five years ago, I was steps away from the danger zone when a roadside bomb exploded. There was carnage everywhere. Three of the guys injured were my friends. I remember frantically moving from one to the other. They were all critical, and I was desperate to help. But I had limited supplies and only two hands. I knew backup wouldn't get there in time to save any of them. So instead of helping someone else who did have a chance of making it, I fell to my knees next to one of the guys who had a young wife and baby at home, held his hand and cried while he died."

Luke's voice choked and he looked away.

Heart aching, Kelsey leaned forward and covered his clenched hands with one of hers. His fingers were ice-cold.

When Luke turned to her, his eyes were haunted. "That was the worst day of my life. I was depressed for weeks, and barely made it through the days. The only way I could survive was to shut down. Stop feeling. I learned to barricade my heart from everyone—including God. To do the job without thinking about personalities. To avoid making friends who could be killed.

"And it worked. It allowed me to cope. I also became the first choice for triage duty. My superiors knew I could make the tough calls, with complete emotional detachment, about who had the best chance of survival. Behind my back, my colleagues called me Doctor Deep Freeze. I was cold and detached and brutally objective in matters of life and death. And I didn't socialize with my peers. I never again wanted to care about anyone enough to feel the way I did when my buddies died from that roadside bomb."

As Luke's mouth settled into a taut line, Kelsey squeezed his clasped hands and spoke in a soft voice.

"The cold, clinical man you're describing isn't the man I know."

He looked down at her hand resting on his. Pulling one of his free, he twined his fingers with hers. "Carlos can take the credit for that. Everyone else steered a wide berth around me, but he sought me out. He'd show up with his tray at mealtimes and try to start a conversation. I'd brush him off, but he'd keep talking. Telling me about his childhood here and his grandmother and his ideas for the youth center. His passion and zest for life eventually won me over. And his zeal for the Lord helped me reconnect with my faith and restore my compassion. But unlocking my heart is still a struggle, Kelsey. I'm afraid if I care too much, I could be hurt again. And the next time I might not make it out of the dark tunnel."

His words roughened, and he cleared his throat as his gaze locked on hers. "I want you to know I've never shared any of this with anyone."

Taken aback, she searched his eyes. "But...why me? We're not much more than acquaintances."

"Because I'd like us to be more than that. And because I trust you. Absolutely."

Overwhelmed, she stared at him, trying to take in the significance of what had just happened.

"I do have one other confession." A tiny smile pulled at one corner of his mouth. "Before she left, Hannah gave me a stern lecture on romance. One of her key points was that if I wanted you to share with me, I had to reciprocate. It's taken me a while to admit my kid sister is right, and longer still to get up the courage to follow her advice. But you know what? I'm glad I did."

Some of the warmth in Kelsey's heart cooled. "You mean…this was all a ploy? A set up? Done with an ulterior motive?"

"If going way outside my comfort zone and letting you in on my biggest fears and secrets—just so you'd know I care—qualifies as an ulterior motive, then I guess I'm guilty as charged."

She picked at a loose thread on the quilt. "And what if I don't want to share mine with you?"

"I still trust you with my secret. And I'll be happy with any positive outcomes." He lifted their entwined hands. "I consider this progress. And for the record, I didn't come over tonight planning to spill my guts like this. But after your phone call, I couldn't walk away. I had to let you know in some meaningful way that I cared. And try to convince you that you can trust me with whatever worries are wrinkling your brow." He reached over and smoothed her forehead with his fingertips, his touch gentle and caring. "Can you at least tell me why the phone call was so upsetting?"

Could she?

Kelsey closed her eyes as she debated that question and fought her own fear. A fear that had morphed from apprehension about her physical safety at their first meeting to one just as frightening in its own right—the fear that, once he knew her story, once she confided her ambivalence on the key question she faced, he might very well walk away. Leaving her feeling lonelier than before.

He would do it compassionately, of course. He'd already made it clear he cared for her. But caring might not cut it. She wasn't even sure loving would, and they weren't anywhere close to that deeper emotion yet.

At the same time, if she didn't tell him, if she shut him out and let him walk away, she'd always wonder what his response might have been.

Besides, in light of his honesty and openness with her, didn't she owe him the same?

Lord, please help me here. Luke's waiting for an answer. Show me what to do.

Chapter Twelve

Luke watched the muscles in Kelsey's face flex, as if she was in pain. He was tempted to tell her to let it go, to forget he'd asked about the call. Whatever her problems, he had a feeling she'd done more than her share of suffering already, and he didn't want to add to her distress.

But if she couldn't trust him after he'd laid his heart bare to her, what future did they have?

So he waited.

At last, the tautness in her features eased and she opened her eyes.

"The call was from a police detective in St. Louis." A tremor ran through her words, and she swallowed. "Beyond that, it's a long story."

Was she telling him that was all she intended to reveal? Or waiting for encouragement to continue?

He chose to assume the latter. Reaching over, he gently touched her collarbone. "Is this scar part of that story?"

"Yes." She drew in a shaky breath. "And so is the baby."

Their fingers were still entwined, and he stroked his thumb over the back of her hand. As long as she was willing to answer his questions, he intended to keep probing. "I've wondered if you might have been involved in an abusive relationship. Or if job stress triggered other problems—like drugs or alcohol—that led you to…do something you later regretted."

"Neither."

His relief at her whispered response was short-lived. Because all at once the pieces fell into place. A traumatized woman easily spooked by a powerful, strong man. A recent scar. A pregnancy that produced ambivalent feelings. A call from the police.

He felt as if someone had kicked him in the stomach.

"You were raped." It wasn't a question.

She gave a jerky nod.

"And the baby…" he glanced at her rounded stomach "…is the result of the attack."

"Yes."

"You decided to carry it to term rather than abort it." He said the words not for confirmation of the obvious, but to try to wrap his mind around her courageous decision.

A tear spilled onto her cheek. "How could I kill an innocent child, Luke?"

"My God." His whispered words were both praise

and awe. "That's the most unselfish thing I've ever heard."

She shook her head. "Don't paint me as a saint, Luke. I did think about taking the easier way out. And there are plenty of days when I wish I'd wake up and all of it would be nothing more than a bad dream."

"But you did the right thing anyway. Even though it was hard." The advice he'd passed on to Hannah years ago replayed in Luke's mind. Kelsey had lived it. Just as she'd lived the values of her faith, not simply paid lip service to them.

She was even more amazing than he'd thought.

Lifting her legs, he slid out from under them, moved beside the couch and dropped to one knee beside her.

At close range, he could see the remembered trauma pooled in the depths of her green eyes. Hear the catch in her irregular breathing. Feel the tremors coursing through her.

All at once, his shock gave way to anger. As he caught and held her fragile fingers, that anger swelled like a tsunami and crashed over him with a power that swept aside every ounce of charity in his soul. "Did they catch the guy?" The hard edge in his question didn't come close to capturing the depth of his outrage and fury.

"That's what tonight's call was about. They have a s-suspect in custody. He was a serial rapist. His latest v-victim inflicted some damage on his face that led to his ID and arrest."

She was shaking now. Badly. Luke stroked her cheek, tucked her hair behind her ear, lifted her hand and brushed his lips across her fingers. All the while fighting the rage surging through him. Kelsey didn't need to see that. What she needed was compassion and support and…love.

"I'm so sorry, Kelsey." His voice hoarsened. "I never imagined anything like this. Have you had counseling?"

"Yes. I still see someone on occasion. It t-took me a long time to get past the shame. And the guilt."

Luke frowned. "There's no shame in being a victim. And why would you feel guilty?"

She blinked the moisture off her lashes. "Because I should have been more careful. I'd heard the news stories about the previous attacks. But I was very disciplined about my exercise routine. So I went jogging as usual that December night after I got home from work, about nine-thirty. It was the route I always used. A public sidewalk that passed a small park. That's where it happened. He always attacked in areas where people were close by. The police said it was a p-power trip for him. That pulling it off in locations where he c-could be detected gave him a thrill."

Squeezing his hand, she closed her eyes. When she continued, her voice was broken, her face shattered. "It all happened s-so fast. He grabbed me from behind as I passed a clump of bushes. Before I could react, he covered my mouth with his hand, pulled a ski headband over my eyes and stuck a k-knife against my throat. He threatened to kill me if I resisted, but I struggled anyway. That's how I got this." She gestured toward her collarbone. "While I was trying to recover from the shock of the cut, he stuffed some rags in my mouth and put plastic restraints around my wrists. It was all over in less than f-five minutes."

She choked on the last word, and a tear rolled down her cheek. Luke brushed it away, his own fingers none too steady. Then he wrapped her in his arms, in a hug that offered comfort and caring and shelter. Much like the one Hannah had given him not long ago.

Pressing her head against his chest, he stroked her back and brushed his lips against her hair as silent tears coursed down her cheeks, dampening his shirt. And she clung to him with a fierceness that revealed the depth of her trauma and her desperate need for a shoulder to cry on.

He would have been happy to hold her that way all night. Absorbing her pain as much as he could. But sooner than he expected, she eased back and looked up at him. Her tear-ravaged face twisted his gut, and he held firm when she tried to disengage, keeping her within the circle of his arms as he scrutinized her. There was some nuance in her expression he didn't understand. Or like.

A red alert went off in his mind, and his stomach clenched. "What is it, Kelsey?"

Her breath came in short gasps and her hands clutched at his back. He was picking up trepidation—and fear—now.

"There's more, Luke."

More? What more could there be? He searched her face, looking for answers, but couldn't get past the fear that was contorting her features. Or the frantic pulse beating in the hollow of her neck.

His arms firmly around her, he braced himself. "Tell me."

She swallowed. Moistened her lips. Tightened her grip on his back. "I'm not sure yet what I'm going to do with the baby."

Her words echoed in the quiet room, and he squinted at her. Had he missed some important piece of information here? "I don't understand. You already made that decision."

"No." She shook her head and caught her lower lip between her teeth. "I mean I haven't decided what I'm going to do with the baby after he or she is born."

Some of his tension eased and he stroked her cheek. "There are plenty of people who can help you with that, Kelsey. Thousands of childless couples are waiting for babies. I'm sure Reverend Howard has connections with adoption agencies. Have you talked with him?"

Another flash of pain ricocheted through her eyes. "Yes. But that's not what I mean."

Confused, he studied her. "Okay. Tell me what you do mean."

She locked gazes with him. "I mean I'm not certain I want to give up the baby."

In the silence that followed Kelsey's bombshell, Luke stared at her. He'd heard her words. But they wouldn't compute. Surely she couldn't mean what he thought she meant.

"Okay." He kept his hands on her arms, absorbing the tremors rippling through her as he tried without much success to slow his own racing pulse. "Are you telling me you're thinking about keeping this baby?"

"Yes." The word came out in a mere whisper.

Luke tried not to panic. Tried not to let go too quickly of the future he was beginning to envision. But that single word changed everything.

A ready-made family was one thing.

Raising as his own a child conceived in violence was another.

How could Kelsey even consider this?

Although he'd done his best to mask his instinctive negative reaction, some of it must have slipped through. Kelsey's irises began to shimmer like deep, green pools, and some fragile quality in their depths died. Hope perhaps. Her features underwent a subtle change, too, and she withdrew a bit, as if pulling in on herself. The change made her look more alone and vulnerable than ever.

He loosened his grip but didn't let her go. He didn't want their relationship to end like this, almost before it had begun. Maybe there was still hope. She hadn't said she'd made a definite decision, just that she was considering keeping the baby. Once she thought through all the ramifications, she might choose adoption after all.

"Kelsey...I'm trying to understand why you'd make that choice. Help me do that."

Her slender shoulders drooped, as if the weight of all that had happened had suddenly become too much to bear. He had the feeling that if he hadn't been holding her arms, keeping her upright, she'd have collapsed back against the pillows.

"I don't know if I can." Her tone was dispirited. Resigned. "Maybe you'd have to be inside my skin to understand." She dipped her head, and he had to lean close to hear her soft response.

"Would you try? Please?"

When she looked up at him, the raw anguish in her eyes tore at his heart.

"In the beginning, I wanted nothing to do with this baby. I wanted to get rid of him or her as fast as I could, once I delivered. But over the months, as I felt this new life stirring inside me, I realized this baby is as much a part of me as it is of him. And I'm not sure I can give up part of myself."

"But won't this child always be a source of bad

memories?" He spoke slowly, even as his mind raced, trying to be empathetic while pointing out the problems he saw. "Won't you relive the violence that gave him or her life every time you look into the child's eyes? Can you offer the kind of love a mother is supposed to give, under the circumstances?"

"I don't know." Her expression grew bleak. "Reverend Howard asked me the same questions. I've been praying for guidance, but so far it hasn't come. All I know is that for a lot of years my priorities were messed up. Nothing mattered to me except my job. My attitude was that if marriage and a family had to be sacrificed on the altar of corporate success, so be it."

She looked over at the wall hanging he'd noticed earlier. "Live. Love. Rejoice."

"The attack changed everything. As horrible as it was, it helped me understand what was important. So I stopped clawing my way up the corporate ladder. I opened a quilt shop, which had always been my secret dream. I hoped that maybe—after a lot of healing—I might meet a man who would want to share my life. But I'm thirty-five, Luke. The biological clock is ticking. The dream of a family seemed remote. After the initial shock of my pregnancy passed, I wondered if God was giving me the gift of family after all. I still wonder that."

That was a stretch, as far as he was concerned. But how could he censure her for taking a horrible trauma and finding good in it?

"You amaze me." He rubbed his hands up and down her chilly arms, finding himself rapidly stepping over the line from friendship to love as he thought of her generous spirit. "Most people in your situation would be bitter."

She attempted a smile, but it flashed and faded as quickly as fireworks in the night sky. "I made a choice to be better, not bitter. I have a long way to go, but that's my goal." Lacing her fingers together in her lap, she looked at him straight on. "So where does this leave us, Luke?"

Good question.

He raked his fingers through his hair and shook his head. "I don't have a clue. I'm still trying to absorb everything you've told me. But I do know one thing. Whatever feelings I had for you when this conversation began are even stronger now." He reached over and stroked his fingers down the gentle curve of her cheek. "I'll tell you what. Why don't we both sleep on this? Regroup tomorrow? Maybe things will be clearer after a good night's rest."

Truth be told, he didn't expect to get much shut-eye tonight. And from the look she gave him, he suspected she felt the same way.

"Okay."

"Now let me take another look at your knee before I leave."

As he flipped back the quilt and stood to remove the ice pack, the shift into doctor mode helped him regain a little of his equilibrium. And a quick inspection reassured him. The swelling was minimal, but the bruise had darkened. "This is going to hurt for a few days."

"I can handle it. I've been through worse."

He thought of the scar near her collarbone. And the other injuries she'd no doubt suffered during the attack. Once more his anger swelled. Despite his years in the line of fire, he'd never been a violent man. Brutality and bloodshed turned his stomach. But if Kelsey's attacker was standing here now, he'd punch the guy out. And he wouldn't suffer one nanosecond of regret.

Needing a few moments to get his anger under control, he resettled the ice pack on her knee, pulled the quilt back into position and picked up her glass and plate.

"Leave those, Luke. I'll take care of them later."

"You need to keep that ice pack on your knee. Besides, I always clean up after myself."

His thoughts more muddled than ever, he made short work of the dishes, wiped down the counter and rejoined her. "Can I do anything else for you tonight?"

Her eyes spoke volumes, communicating a need that had nothing to do with practical assistance, but she just shook her head.

"Call me if anything comes up, okay?"

She acknowledged his request with a dip of her head.

It was time to go. But all at once he felt as if he was running out on her.

She seemed to sense his dilemma. "Go home, Luke. I think we both need some time and distance to digest everything."

"Yeah." He shoved his hands into his pockets. A shaft of light from the setting sun was gilding her blond hair and turning her pale skin golden. Her lips were slightly parted, her eyes wide, her chin firm— and resolute. She was both strong and vulnerable, and despite his uncertainty about what lay ahead, he couldn't resist the appeal of that juxtaposition.

Crossing the room, he stopped beside her, bent down and brushed his lips over the satiny skin of her forehead. "Good night, Kelsey."

"'Night."

Her strangled response caught on a sob, and he was tempted to stay. To tell her everything was fine, that what she'd told him tonight hadn't changed a thing.

But that was a lie. It had.

With a final squeeze of her hand, he strode from the room, collected the artist's renderings from the screened porch, and headed across the lawn toward his house.

Before he'd visited Kelsey tonight, Luke had made his peace—to some degree—with the notion of a ready-made family.

A child born of violence, however...that was a different story.

He paused, watching the setting sun edge the ominous black clouds in the distance with gold, transforming them into a thing of beauty. That's what Kelsey was trying to do—make something beautiful out of a storm. And perhaps she'd succeed. Perhaps she'd eventually find it in her heart to accept this child on his or her own merits. Maybe a mother's love would be strong enough to overcome her memories of the baby's traumatic conception.

From what he'd seen of Kelsey's kind heart, loving spirit and positive attitude, she just might be able to pull it off.

But as a distant rumble of thunder prodded him toward his own house, he wasn't sure he could do the same.

Long after Luke left, Kelsey remained on the couch. The sun had set, taking with it the glow that had illuminated the room earlier, when Luke had been with her. Now it was dark.

She ought to get up. Put on some lights. Try to chase away the gloom.

Besides, she'd promised Detective Layton she'd check her email.

In truth, that latter task was the main reason she hadn't moved. She didn't want to look at the man who had turned her life upside down.

But it had to be done.

Removing the icc pack from her knee, Kelsey tugged the quilt off her legs and swung her feet to the floor. The move was less than graceful, thanks to her girth, and her knee protested when she bent it.

She reached up to turn on the lamp beside the couch, and a quick inspection told her Luke hadn't been exaggerating about the bruising. Her whole kneecap was purple. At least the ice had kept the swelling down.

With one hand on the arm of the couch and the other on the seat, Kelsey managed to maneuver herself to her feet. She tested her knee, wincing when she put weight on it, but by holding on to the walls and furniture, she managed to limp into the quilt room where she kept her computer.

Instead of sitting, she bent over the keyboard, clicked on her desktop email icon and typed in her password. A quick scan of unopened mail told her Detective Layton had followed through. A JPEG was attached.

Opening the email, she moved the mouse to the JPEG file. Froze.

Just do it, Kelsey!

She double clicked, then clicked Open at the prompt. Two seconds later, a headshot filled the screen.

Her attacker.

Her baby's father.

The breath jammed in her throat, and her world tilted. She gripped the back of the desk chair. Made herself breathe.

With a triumph of will over emotion, she forced herself to look at the photo long enough to note the man's brown eyes and stringy, dark-brown hair. To trace the long scar that started on his cheek and disappeared into his hairline. To examine a chin that was too pointed and thin lips that curled into a smirk.

And to know she'd never seen him before.

Fingers trembling, she closed the window and typed in a four-word reply to Detective Layton:

"I don't know him."

She hit Send. Selected his email. Hit Delete.

The message and the photo disappeared from her in-box.

If only she could delete the trauma as easily from her memory.

Her emotions in tatters, she limped back down the hall toward the kitchen. She needed a glass of water and another Tylenol. Then she was going to go to bed. And pray sleep would come, bringing peace. And clarity.

As she drew a glass of water at the tap, she surveyed the familiar kitchen where she and Gram had spent so many happy hours. From the time her mother died, this little cottage had always been the symbol of comfort and love for Kelsey.

Tonight, that symbolism had been reinforced.

Thanks to Luke.

But after his reaction to her story, she was afraid

his offer of comfort—and perhaps love— might be short-lived.

In all honesty, she couldn't blame him if he backtracked. If *she* was on the fence about whether to keep the baby after carrying her child close to her heart all these months, how could she expect Luke to embrace the prospect?

As she set the glass on the counter, she looked out the window. Through the branches of the trees, she could see a light burning on Luke's deck. He must be out there. Thinking about what had transpired tonight. Wondering how—or if—their futures were destined to entwine.

Heart aching, she turned away and headed toward the hall. On the threshold, she paused and gave the pristine kitchen one more inspection. Luke had done a good job cleaning up the mess he'd made.

In her kitchen, if not her heart.

Chapter Thirteen

Kelsey peered bleary-eyed at the digital clock on her nightstand. Three-fourteen in the morning. And her knee was still throbbing.

But that wasn't what had awakened her

She had a cramp in her stomach.

Grimacing, she turned on her side, seeking a more comfortable position. Not that she'd been able to find one for the past six hours. Luke's visit last night had further frayed her already tattered emotions and left her stressed and edgy.

No wonder she was having stomach pains.

Just as she began to drift off to sleep, another cramp pulled her back to wakefulness. Only it didn't exactly feel like a cramp. It felt more like…a contraction?

Kelsey's fingers clenched on the sheet and a spurt of adrenaline drove away every vestige of sleep. She'd been doing some research on labor and knew Braxton Hicks contractions could be expected at this stage of her pregnancy. She hadn't yet experienced them, but that last twinge had felt a lot like the sensation described in the material she'd read.

Struggling into a sitting position, she propped her back against the headboard. Too bad she and Dorothy hadn't signed up for an earlier childbirth class. Braxton Hicks contractions were probably covered in great detail. But they'd only completed the first session of the three-week class that met on Tuesday evenings. Session Two wasn't until next week.

As the minutes ticked by with no further incident, the soft light from the lamp on her dresser lulled her back toward sleep. Okay. Good. Everything was fine. She'd just overreacted because she was on edge.

Her eyelids grew heavy, and she blinked. Yawned. When the time came, she'd…

Wham!

Another contraction tightened her abdominal muscles, and her eyes flew open.

This wasn't stress-related.

It must be Braxton Hicks, after all.

Kelsey eased her legs over the edge of the bed and stood, trying to remain calm as she searched her memory for some nuggets from her research on Braxton Hicks. The contractions were irregular. She recalled reading that. And unpredictable. Changing position was also supposed to make them stop or slow down.

Right.

Okay. She'd walk around a little. Get a drink of

water. Once they stopped, she'd go back to bed and try to salvage what was left of this night.

Good plan.

Except halfway down the hall to the kitchen another contraction stole her breath.

Panic nibbled at her composure as she continued toward the kitchen, flipped on a light and groped through a drawer for a pad of paper and pen. She'd time a few contractions. That would tell her a lot. Prove she didn't need to worry.

She settled on a stool to wait, trying to ignore the tremble in her fingers as she noted the hour, minute and second on the pad of paper.

Six minutes and forty seconds later, she gripped the edge of the counter as another contraction hit. According to the second hand on her watch, it lasted thirty-five seconds. But it wasn't all that painful. Surely not strong enough to be real labor. It felt more like a bad case of indigestion. Besides, she wasn't due for another four-plus weeks.

Time to change position again, move around. She needed to get rid of these things so she could go back to bed and try to sleep.

For a few minutes she wandered through the house, favoring her sore knee. She picked up a newspaper and disposed of it. Straightened a picture on the wall. Wiped down the counter again.

Just when she began to believe the contractions were history, another one rolled over her. Six minutes and twenty-two seconds since the last one, according to her watch. It, too, lasted thirty-five seconds.

This wasn't good.

But she wasn't going to jump to conclusions. Until there was a definite pattern, she didn't intend to call Dr. Evans.

Resettling herself on the kitchen stool, she picked up the pen and waited.

Forty-five minutes later, after tracking seven contractions that were now coming every five and a half minutes and lasting forty seconds, she accepted reality.

This baby was coming. Ready or not.

Not being the operative word.

Fingers fumbling with the phone, she tapped in Dr. Evans's exchange and left a message. Four minutes later, the OB called her back and listened as Kelsey gave her a recap.

"It's possible we're still dealing with Braxton Hicks, but all indications are you're in the late stages of the early phase of labor. You need to get to the hospital so we can check this out."

"I don't even have a bag packed yet." Kelsey combed her fingers through her hair, her mind refusing to accept the reality. "And it's too soon. The baby's not due for almost five weeks." *And I haven't decided what to do with it yet!*

"Babies don't always abide by our rules. As for the bag, don't waste time packing. The hospital will have everything you need for the immediate future.

I'll alert them you're coming. And I'll meet you there if things progress."

As Kelsey ended the call, another contraction gripped her. Once it passed, she headed for the bedroom to throw on some clothes. Dorothy had planned to drive her to the hospital in Holland when the time came, but the older woman had had a date with Charles last night. She couldn't wake her at this hour. Besides, the pains weren't that bad. She could cope long enough to drive herself. It wasn't far.

In less than five minutes, Kelsey was dressed and out the door. The breeze off the lake was cool, and she shivered as she headed for the detached garage in the dark, wishing she'd grabbed a warmer sweater.

Halfway there, she had to stop as another contraction took hold. They were growing progressively more intense, but they were still manageable. And at this hour, foot to the floor, she could get to the hospital in Holland in less than fifteen minutes. The facility was only three contractions away.

She could make it.

As her abdominal muscles relaxed, she struck out for the garage again. But a sudden, odd gushing sensation brought her to an abrupt stop.

It was too dark to see what had happened, but she could feel it in the biting chill from the wind as it hit the damp fabric clinging to her legs.

Her water had broken.

This baby was coming.

Now.

Fear gripped her lungs in a vise, cutting off her breath.

No way could she drive now. And she might not have time to wait for Dorothy, if she did rouse the older woman. There was always 911, though the notion of an ambulance ride didn't sit well with her.

That left only one option.

She glanced at Luke's dark house through the trees, hesitating. He might not appreciate being pulled into this mess, considering his reaction to her story last night. But he was a doctor. And he was steps away. It was logical to ask for his help.

Yet logic wasn't the catalyst that sent her stumbling toward his house in the dark. It was a decision of the heart.

Because Kelsey was scared. And she wanted him to hold her hand.

The pounding on his back door brought Luke instantly awake, a souvenir of his frontline experience that he expected would be with him for years to come.

Groping for his jeans in the dark, he checked the bedside clock. Four-twenty. Either someone was very drunk—or in big trouble. He grabbed a T-shirt and pulled it over his head as he strode barefoot down the hall toward the kitchen.

One look through the window as he drew close gave him his answer.

Someone was in big trouble.

Kelsey.

Adrenaline surging, he flipped on the deck light, unbolted the door and yanked it open. She spoke before he could ask the obvious question, hysteria raising the pitch of her voice.

"The baby's c-coming. My w-water broke. I was going to d-drive myself, but…" She gasped and grabbed for the door frame to steady herself, her features tightening with pain.

Shoving the door aside with his shoulder, Luke slid an arm under her knees and lifted her against his chest. He ignored the dampness seeping into his T-shirt and held her close as she shivered.

"It's okay, Kelsey. I'm here. Hold on to me."

She needed no encouragement. Clutching his T-shirt, she bunched it into her fists and buried her face against his chest, her breath coming in short, ragged gasps.

It was the longest sixty seconds of his life.

When the contraction released her, the tension in her muscles eased. But her shaking continued unabated.

After setting her gently in a kitchen chair with a reassurance he'd be right back, Luke retrieved a blanket from the hall closet. He draped it around her shoulders, then dropped to one knee beside her and took her hands. Her eyes were wide with panic, and she gripped his fingers as if she'd never let go.

"We'll deal with this, okay?" He used his best bedside manner, striving to instill confidence by appearing to be in total control. She didn't need to know his insides were quaking just as they had the day his three buddies had been killed by the roadside bomb. And the day Carlos had died. "Kelsey?"

She sucked in a breath. "Okay."

"Did you call your doctor?"

"Yes. She told me to go to the hospital."

"Did you time the contractions?"

"Yes. They're five minutes apart and last about a minute. And they're getting stronger."

"Okay. We'll take my car."

He snatched his keys off the counter, grabbed a pillow and more blankets from the bedroom and rejoined her in the kitchen. "Give me two minutes to put these in the car."

Ninety second later, he returned to find her huddled in the chair, still shaking. She looked up when he entered, her eyes wide with fright.

"It's too soon, Luke."

"Babies are born early all the time, Kelsey. You're less than five weeks from your due date. You're early, but not dangerously early."

"But I… I'm not ready. I haven't decided…" All at once she gripped her midsection.

Luke went down on one knee beside her again, putting them at eye level. "Look at me, Kelsey."

Once he had her attention, he continued, his voice soft but firm. "Focus on my eyes and breathe with me. Come on, you can do this. In through the nose, out through the mouth." He drew in a long breath. She did the same. He held it for a few seconds, then exhaled slowly. She mimicked his actions. He repeated that exercise until the contraction passed.

"Okay. Let's get to the hospital." He stood and helped her to her feet. "Can you walk, or do you want me to carry you?"

"I'll walk. I don't want to give you a h-hernia."

Despite her fear, despite her panic, she was trying to make a joke.

She was one gutsy gal.

Once he had her in the car, he slid behind the wheel and started the engine. As he backed out, her sharp intake of breath told him another contraction was beginning. He glanced at his watch before pulling onto the main road.

"Kelsey, I want you to picture a rosebud and I want you to imagine it opening one petal at a time while you take some deep breaths."

"Okay." The word came out in a gasp.

"All right. Take in a long, slow breath through your nose to the count of five, hold it five, let it out through your mouth in five. Here we go." He kept tabs on her shadowy figure in the backseat as he counted, repeating the process over and over until the contraction ended. Sixty-two seconds.

She was definitely in the second stage of labor.

"That one was worse." Her voice hiccupped.

"Have you taken any childbirth classes?" It didn't much matter at this point, but he wanted to keep her distracted. Focused on something besides the pain and fear.

"I signed up for the evening class. Dorothy and I only made it to the first one. Last week."

"Dorothy?" He pulled onto I-196 and floored it.

"She was going to be my labor coach."

Luke couldn't picture the proper, every-hair-in-place, pearl-wearing older woman in that role. But if that's who Kelsey wanted… "Would you like me to call her for you?"

No response.

He flicked another look in the rearview mirror. "Kelsey?"

"She's not…prepared for this."

Neither was the occupant of his backseat. But he left that unsaid.

"Tell me what you learned in the first class."

She recounted what she recalled from the session, but halfway through she stopped. "Another one is coming."

Luke checked his watch. Only four minutes since the last contraction. Things were moving quickly.

Too quickly.

"Okay. We're going to do the same thing we did the last time."

Once more, he walked her through the contraction. Wishing he could hold her hand. Absorb some of her pain. Ease her mind about the looming decision she wasn't yet ready to make.

By the time it ended he was exiting the highway at Holland. "We're almost there, Kelsey. Try to relax as much as you can."

"That's easy for you to say."

He caught the whisper of a tease under the strain in her voice. Good for her.

Although he hadn't been to the hospital in Holland, he'd driven by it on his way to meetings with potential supporters of the youth center project. And since the streets were deserted at this hour, he made good time. Still, as he pulled into the E.R. entrance, another contraction hit.

After setting the brake, he slid out of the car, opened her door and took her hand. He crouched beside her, half in and half out of the car, and as she took his fingers in a fierce grasp, her features contorted.

"Watch me, Kelsey. Concentrate on my face. Breathe with me."

Though her eyes were hazy with pain, she hung in with him, doing her best to follow his instructions.

Once it passed, she sagged against the pillow wedged behind her. He brushed her hair away from her damp forehead, then touched her cheek. "I'll be right back with a wheelchair."

Without waiting for a reply, he backed out of the car and jogged toward the entrance. They needed to get her to a room and prepped fast. Because, based on the rapid progression of her labor, this baby was coming fast.

Very fast.

As Kelsey waited in the car for Luke to return, she was too limp to do more than lie there like a rag doll. But her mind was racing.

All her life she'd been a planner. In both business and personal matters, she'd always thought ahead, prepared for contingencies, done her best to avoid surprises or last-minute decisions.

But she'd blown it with this baby.

Now, under the most stressful circumstances, with pain dulling her usual clear, precise thought processes, she'd have to make a choice about the future of this baby that would affect her future as well. For the rest of her life.

And she wasn't ready to do that.

The pain was building again, and she pressed her hands against her stomach, bracing.

God, please…show me the way! Help me make the right decision!

Suddenly Luke was beside her again, his voice calm, his gaze steady as he talked her through the contraction. She liked focusing on his face better than picturing an unfurling rose. Those dark brown eyes sucked her in, and she let herself fall into their caring depths, concentrating on the man in front of her and the breathing he was coaching her through.

The instant the pain subsided, though, he stood and motioned to the aide with the wheelchair. With their assistance, she eased into it and was rolled inside.

Whatever Luke had told them when he'd gone to retrieve the wheelchair had galvanized the staff. They didn't stop at the desk, but headed straight for the birth center. She was wheeled into a private birthing room where a nurse was waiting. The woman already knew Luke was a physician, because she called him Dr. Turner.

Just as the aide rolled her up to the bed, another contraction took hold.

There was a muted, clipped exchange between Luke and the nurse. A moment later he lifted her onto the bed and took her hand, coaching her through the pain again.

When it ended, he moved aside to make room for the nurse.

"Hi, Kelsey. I'm Sandra, and I'll be with you until this baby decides to arrive. I need to do a preliminary evaluation to see how far along you are, then I'll check the baby's heart and help you change into a gown."

The nurse went to retrieve some latex gloves, and Luke released her hand and stepped back. "I'll wait outside."

As he turned away, panic clawed at Kelsey's throat. "Luke!"

At her call, he angled back toward her.

She bunched the sheet in her fingers, torn. She shouldn't ask him to stay. He had things to do. The baby wasn't his. In fact, her child was a stumbling block to their relationship.

But she desperately needed his gentle touch. His quiet confidence. His steady support. Without it, she didn't know how she'd get through the next few hours.

As if reading her mind, he moved to the foot of the bed. "Would you like me to stay until the baby is born, Kelsey?"

"Yes." Warmth and gratitude spilled out of her heart as she whispered the response.

"Then I'll be here."

The nurse returned to the bed and glanced at him. "Give us five minutes."

With a nod, he exited.

She missed him immediately.

Sandra chatted with her during the exam and while she helped her change, assuring her the baby was doing fine. But Kelsey's mind wasn't on that conversation. It was on the kind, compassionate army doctor who had taken up residence next door—and in her heart.

A man who might be poised to play a starring role in her future.

Yet much could depend on the momentous decision she faced. A decision that had been thrust on her far sooner than anticipated. Nor was this the way she'd planned to make it—under stress and in crisis mode. But as she well knew, her plans didn't always mesh with God's.

All she could do was put herself in His hands and pray for wisdom and guidance in the hours to come.

Chapter Fourteen

Hands in the pockets of his jeans, Luke paced the hall outside Kelsey's room, waiting for the nurse to summon him back inside. After the bombshell she'd dropped last evening, he hadn't managed to clock more than two hours of sleep. Instead, he'd spent the dark hours tossing as he'd grappled with the implications of the choice before her—and prayed she'd make the one that would clear the path for their friendship to transition to something deeper.

Because as the long night had dragged by minute by agonizing minute, he'd become more and more convinced he could never accept as his own the child she carried. Every time he looked at her son and daughter he'd think of the man who'd brutalized the woman who was stealing his heart. That, in turn, would lead to feelings of anger and resentment instead of love. Feelings a child could pick up. And he feared Kelsey would have the same problem.

All of which had convinced him that everyone

would be best served if the child was adopted by a couple who had no baggage and could offer the baby the unconditional love it deserved.

The only bright spot in his long night had been the hope that in the month before the child was born, he could persuade Kelsey to see the logic of his reasoning.

But now that opportunity had been snatched from him. The baby was coming and Kelsey would be forced to make her decision under less than ideal circumstances.

He closed his eyes and wearily propped a shoulder against the wall.

Why, Lord?

The silent question echoed in his mind, unanswered, leaving him confused, bereft and frustrated. He tried to find some redeeming value in the situation, but if there was any, it eluded him. He hadn't a clue why the Lord would bring a woman like Kelsey into his life, then set up roadblocks on the path to romance.

"You look like you could use some caffeine."

He turned, and a smiling aide extended a disposable cup of coffee toward him. Considering the day's worth of stubble on his face, his uncombed hair and his stained T-shirt, he figured that was a gross understatement.

"Thank you." He reached for it and took a gulp of the strong brew.

"Long night?"

"Yeah."

"Is this your first?"

He blinked, uncomprehending for a moment. Then her meaning registered. "I'm not the father. I'm a…friend."

If the misstep embarrassed the woman, she didn't let on. "Friends are good, too. Sometimes more helpful than fathers, to be honest. A lot of *them* are basket cases." She winked and motioned toward a doorway behind her. "There's a pot of coffee in there if you need more."

"Thanks."

With a nod, she headed down the hall.

"Dr. Turner?" The nurse stuck her head out of the door behind him. "Kelsey needs her coach."

Downing another swig of the hot brew, he followed the woman back inside.

Even before he checked the readout from the sensor that had been attached to Kelsey's stomach, he knew this contraction was bad. She was gasping, every muscle taut, and her grip was crushing as he set his coffee on the bedside table and took her hand.

"I'm here, Kelsey." He got up close to her face. "Look at me, sweetheart. Look at my eyes. We'll breathe together."

She tried. Hard. He could see the effort she was making to focus on him. But it was becoming more difficult for her to distance herself from the pain.

By the time the contraction ended, she was shaking and shivering.

Smoothing the hair away from her forehead as she collapsed against the pillow, he spoke to the nurse. "How far along is she?"

"The cervix is anterior and seventy-five percent effaced. It's at seven centimeters."

"Have you called her OB?"

"I'm going to do that now."

"She could use a warm blanket."

"On my list."

As the woman exited, Kelsey opened her eyes. "Wow." The word came out in a weak rush of breath.

"You're doing great." He leaned closer and touched her cheek again. "But if you want an epidural, we need to move fast. You're already past the usual stage for one. As it is, they might have to use a spinal block."

Her brow wrinkled. "What do you think I should do?"

He was tempted to tell her to go for it. Watching her suffer was eating at his gut. But professionally, he had a different opinion.

"This isn't my specialty, Kelsey. But there are potential complications with pain medication—for both you and the baby. Your blood pressure could drop without warning, which would affect blood flow to the baby. Pushing will be more difficult, so forceps may have to be used. Sometimes a doctor will have to go the cesarean route. And there are other issues—all relatively rare, but real. It comes down to how well you think you can hold up."

She caught her lower lip between her teeth. "How much longer could this go on?"

"The rule of thumb is one centimeter an hour. You have three to go. But you're progressing a lot faster than that. Unusual for a first baby, but not unheard of."

"How fast?"

"You're very close to the transition phase. That's the most intense part of labor. The contractions will be coming faster and stronger."

"Wow."

The monitor caught his eye, and he took her hand again. "Here comes another one. Get ready."

Luke talked her through the contraction, wondering what she would decide about pain medication, prepared to support her whatever her choice.

But in the end, the decision was taken out of her hands.

Over the next fifteen minutes, her contractions started coming every two minutes and lasting more than a minute. She had little chance to recover in between. Her OB arrived, Kelsey was prepped for delivery, and after an intense period of pushing, the baby's head, topped with damp blond hair, crowned.

She was panting now, under his direction, her focus on the mirror positioned so she could see her baby's arrival. Luke found himself mesmerized, too. The forehead appeared. The nose. The mouth. The chin. The shoulders emerged, one at a time.

And then, with one final push, the baby slid into the doctor's waiting hands.

"You have a daughter, Kelsey." As the doctor passed on the news, she suctioned the baby's mouth and nasal passages.

Kelsey was still clinging to his hand, shaking, and Luke squeezed her fingers, motioning to the nurse. "We need another warm blanket."

Seconds later, the woman handed him one and he draped it over Kelsey.

"It's a girl, Luke." Her voice was filled with awe, her face awash with the wonder of the miracle they'd just witnessed.

He smoothed back her hair. "I know."

"Is she all right?"

"She's fine, Kelsey." The OB spoke from the foot of the bed. "On the small side, but looking good. Do you want to cut the cord?"

"No. I—I'm too shaky."

The doctor took care of the procedure as she continued talking. "After we check her out you can hold her. Meanwhile, we've still got to deliver the placenta. Hang in there for another few minutes, okay?"

Luke doubted Kelsey even heard the doctor's last comment. Her attention was riveted on the tiny bundle of life the nurse was weighing and measuring a few feet away. The new arrival was waving her fists and already displaying an impressive set of lungs as she howled in protest about leaving the warm cocoon that had been her safe, protected haven for almost eight months.

"Why is she crying?" Kelsey tensed, straining to get a better view of the baby. "Is something wrong?"

"No. She's just announcing her arrival," Dr. Evans responded. "But we'll have a neonatal specialist check her out after you two say hello."

"Four-point-eight pounds, seventeen inches," the nurse announced as she picked up the squalling baby and moved next to Kelsey. "Okay, Mom, here we go."

Bending over Kelsey, the woman positioned the kicking baby on her stomach. After covering the tiny infant with a warm blanket, she tugged a pink cap over the damp, golden ringlets, leaving a few curls to peek out.

Luke heard Kelsey's breath catch as she looked at the baby. Reaching out a tentative hand, she stroked a trembling finger down the infant's spindly arm, which was more bone than flesh at this stage of development. Big blue eyes, fringed by thick lashes clumped with tears, stared back at her. Then the baby grabbed Kelsey's finger with a tiny fist and held tight. A few moments later, her sobs morphed into snuffles. She stopped quivering and lay on Kelsey's stomach, quietly watching her mom.

As Luke transferred his gaze from the baby to Kelsey, the air whooshed out of his lungs. The serenity of her expression, the absolute peace in her eyes, told him she'd made her decision.

There was no way she was giving up this baby.

Even if that meant there was no future for them.

She was beautiful. Perfect. Sweetness incarnate. And a gift from God.

As her baby held tight to her finger, Kelsey realized her prayers had been answered. She'd asked for guidance about what to do with this baby. Had worried she'd never be able to love this child, the product of a brutal crime. But all along God had known that once she laid eyes on the daughter who had grown within her, she'd never be able to let her go. Maybe that's why He'd let her come early—to save Kelsey the agony of wrestling with a decision that was so clear-cut in hindsight.

"Does this little lady have a name, Mom?" Sandra smiled at Kelsey.

Dr. Evans looked up, as if to intervene. Her OB knew the story of the baby's conception, knew Kelsey had been thinking about putting her child up for adoption. But Kelsey answered first.

"Yes, she does. It's Grace. Grace Elizabeth."

That, too, had come without forethought. Grace wasn't a product of the baby name book she'd perused. Nor a tribute to some beloved family member. It was a reflection of what this child had meant to her. For out of an act of violence, God had showered her with grace and redeemed her life.

But the middle name *was* a tribute. To Gram—and her example of strength and independence, which had given Kelsey the courage to follow a new path after her world was turned upside down.

The nurse smiled. "That's lovely. And it suits her."

"Would you like me to recommend a pediatrician, Kelsey?" Dr. Evans asked, stripping off her gloves as she rose.

"Yes. Thank you."

The OB moved beside her. "You haven't asked, but everything went fine with the delivery. No complications, and very few restrictions on activity once you're released in a couple of days. We'll want to keep Grace a bit longer, since she's mildly premature, to make sure she can maintain body temperature, eat and gain weight. A week, maybe. But her doctor will decide that. Now it's off to the nursery for you, young lady."

She motioned to Sandra, who wheeled a crib enclosed in plastic next to the bed.

"Are you planning on breast-feeding?" The nurse lifted the baby, gently disengaging her from Kelsey's finger. Grace's face crumpled and she let out a howl of protest.

Kelsey's heart contracted as the woman settled Grace in the crib. She understood how her daughter

felt. She, too, wanted to howl at the separation. Bu
at least it was only temporary.

"Yes, I am." That, too, was a spur-of-the-momen
decision. But it felt right. And at this point Kelsey
was winging it, following her heart, riding on a
sudden wave of euphoria.

"I'll have a lactation consultant come in and tall
with you."

Kelsey watched Sandra wheel Grace away as Dr
Evans moved back beside the bed.

"You did great, Kelsey. And so did your coach."
She smiled and reached a hand across the bed. "I
was nice to meet you, Dr. Turner."

Kelsey's eyes flew open. Luke! She'd forgotte
all about him! Twisting her head, she watched hin
shake hands with the OB.

"And good luck with the youth center project," D
Evans continued. "My husband and I have alread
purchased tickets to the dinner auction. I hope it'
a resounding success."

"Thank you."

"Ring if you need anything, Kelsey. I'll be bac
to check on you later today."

With that, the doctor strode toward the door, leav
ing her with the man whose warm, brown eyes ha
coaxed her through the pain. Whose firm clasp ha
given her a lifeline to cling to during the rocky rid
Whose gentle touches and encouragement had no
only comforted her, but touched her heart and mad
her feel less alone, if only for a few hours.

No way could Dorothy have accomplished all that during her intense labor, much as Kelsey loved the older woman.

Her eyes misted, and she twined her fingers through his. "How can I ever thank you? You were my rock. I couldn't have done it without you."

One side of his mouth hitched up. "Yes, you could. Babies come, no matter what."

She conceded the point with a slight lift of her shoulders. "True. But I couldn't have done it as gracefully without you." She squinted, trying to remember the past few hours, but they were all a blur. "Or *did* I do it gracefully? I didn't yell at you or anything, did I?"

"Actually, my ears are still ringing."

Her mouth dropped open. "Are you serious?"

He chuckled. "No. You were a champ."

"Really?"

"Yeah. Really." He tugged his fingers free, glanced at his watch and moved to the bottom of the bed. "Listen, I need to go home and clean up. Will you be okay by yourself? The call button is right there if you need anything." He gestured to where the nurse had pinned it to the blanket.

Kelsey surveyed him. He did look in desperate need of a shower, shave and change of clothes. But she also sensed the distance he'd put between them was more than physical. His eyes were still warm and caring. But now that the crisis was over, there was a touch of reserve in them. As if he'd withdrawn a bit.

And the reason was obvious—her decision to keep Grace.

She'd known last night that he had serious reservations about such a choice. And he'd had less than twenty-four hours to digest everything she'd thrown at him. Maybe he just needed some time to think things through. After all, no matter the circumstances of her conception, how could anyone look at Grace's sweet innocence and not fall in love with her? While Luke didn't have the connection to her that she had, he did have a compassionate and kind heart. He could learn to care for Grace. Her daughter didn't have to be a deal breaker.

Did she?

"Kelsey? Will you be okay?"

She'd never answered his question.

"Yes. Fine. Thank you again for everything."

She wanted to ask when she'd see him again. But she bit back the question, not certain she wanted to hear the answer.

"Okay. Call if you need anything."

"I will." She summoned up a smile. "But I've got other reinforcements I can muster, too. I'm going to call my sister as soon as you leave. She said she'd come and stay for a few days if… When the baby was born. And Dorothy will help."

"Sounds like you've got it covered."

Not even close.

But he was talking about practical issues, not matters of the heart.

"I'll be fine, Luke." Her artificially cheerful tone came out a bit too bright. "You don't need to worry."

He hesitated, as if he wanted to say more. But in the end he nodded, turned and walked out the door.

And short of a miracle, she had a feeling that in sixteen days he was going to walk out of her life as well.

Perhaps forever.

His phone was ringing.

At some subconscious level, Luke's brain registered the sound and identified it. But translating that awareness into action was proving difficult. After coming home, getting cleaned up and heading into town for the late Sunday morning service, the stress of last night—and the lack of sleep—had hit him. He'd crashed on the couch, out almost before he hit the cushions.

He had no idea what time it was now. And he didn't care. All he wanted to do was sleep.

The cell phone went silent, and he started to drift off.

Thirty seconds later, it rang again.

Groaning, Luke draped a hand over his forehead, pried his eyes open and squinted at his watch. Four-thirty. He'd been out for three hours. Not enough.

The cell went silent again. The ring had been muted, and it took him a minute to realize the phone had slipped off his belt and fallen between the cushions on the sofa. He dug it out, planning to check his voicemail, when it rang again.

Someone really wanted to reach him.

Kelsey?

His pulse kicked up a notch, but a quick check of caller ID relieved his mind. It was Hannah.

"Missing me already?" He swung his feet to the floor, stifling a yawn as he sat.

"Very funny. Listen, I have some news."

The undercurrent of excitement in her voice piqued his interest. "What's up?"

"You'll never guess who tweeted me last night! Well, not me directly. Carlos."

At she rattled off the name of a Grammy-award-winning singer, Luke's eyebrows rose. "That's impressive. What did she say?"

"That she was touched by the story about the fundraiser and was going to check out the website. And get this—our number of followers has *tripled* since then! That should mean more contributions. But I have even better news. I sent her a private tweet in response, and she got back in touch after she looked at the website. She said she was going to be doing a concert in Grand Rapids the day after the dinner, and she was willing to stop in at the auction and do a couple of songs! I sent her your cell number. She's going to call you. Isn't that fabulous?"

It was more than fabulous. Over the past few weeks, Luke's work with Kelsey on PR for the youth center project had taught him the value of this kind of publicity. With a name like that aligned with their cause, they'd have no problem selling every seat at the dinner and generating national coverage for the event. All of which should translate into a big boost in their efforts to raise enough dollars to turn Carlos's dream into a reality.

"It's amazing." Luke leaned back against the couch and stared out the window at the deep blue sky, cloudless on this mid-August day. "You know, if you and Kelsey hadn't jumped on board, the youth center project would still be just a local fundraiser that might or might not get us where we need to be."

"I didn't do much. Setting up the Twitter page was easy. Kelsey's done the real publicity work. I tried to call her a bunch of times to share my news, but she's not answering or returning my calls."

"That's because she's been busy having a baby."

Dead silence greeted that announcement, followed by an explosive response.

"But she's not due for weeks! Is she okay? Is the baby okay? What did she have? Has she picked a name? When is she—"

"Whoa! One question at a time. Everyone is fine. The baby's name is Grace Elizabeth."

"Grace Elizabeth. I like it. Wow. This is so cool!"

Luke could think of other ways to describe it, bu
he remained silent.

"So have you seen her?" Hannah prodded.

"Yes."

"And…?"

"And what?"

"Come on, Luke! I want details. Is she ecstatic
Is the baby cute?"

He thought about the look of luminous joy o
Kelsey's face as she'd gazed at her new daughte
Pictured the big, blue eyes of the baby, fixated o
her mother, and the blond ringlets.

"Yes to both."

She huffed out a frustrated breath. "Boy, it's lik
pulling teeth to get information from you. I'll ju
have to call her directly. Where is she?"

"Holland Hospital."

"Got it. When are you going to see her again?"

"I don't know, Hannah."

In the silence that followed, he could imagine th
gears turning in his sister's head. Could visuali
her eyes narrowing.

"What's that supposed to mean?"

He raked his fingers through his hair. "It mea
things are complicated."

"They don't have to be."

For all her maturity, Luke knew his sister sti
harbored juvenile romantic fantasies. But real li
didn't come with happy endings all neatly tied u
with ribbon.

"It's more complicated than you think, Hannah."

"Why? Did the baby's father show up?"

"No. And he won't."

"O-kaaay. You obviously know more about that than you're telling. That's fine. I'm not going to pry. But if the father's out of the picture, what's the big problem?"

"Geography. And don't start on the long-distance courtship thing again. That's a manageable short-term problem. Think long-term. My job is in Atlanta. A job I am very much looking forward to. Kelsey's life and her work are here. She wouldn't want to leave Michigan."

"How do you know? Have you asked her?"

"No. It would be a little premature for that. But I know how much she loves this place. I can't see her leaving."

"You know, before you write her off for that—*if* that's the main reason—you might want to have a little chat with her on the subject."

A frown creased Luke's brow. "What do you know that I don't know?"

"Ask her yourself. I wouldn't want to betray any confidences. In the meantime, you better check your messages. I bet you'll find one from a very well-known singer. And now I'm calling Kelsey to give her the news and get some *details* on her and the baby. Talk to you later, Luke."

The line went dead.

His mind occupied with Hannah's comments

about Kelsey, Luke shifted into autopilot and followed his sister's instruction to check his messages. Most were from Hannah. But sure enough, the pop star had also left a message. And her phone number.

If they could actually work out the logistics, it would be a bonanza. One they needed to milk from every possible angle. And that required very special expertise. The kind Kelsey possessed.

Sliding the phone back onto his belt, Luke rose and wandered out to the deck. He needed Kelsey. And not just for the youth center project. Watching her last night, scared out of her mind but somehow managing to insert touches of humor into the situation, he'd known this was the kind of woman he wanted by his side in good times and bad. She'd had more adversity in the past year than most people endured in a lifetime, yet she hadn't let it destroy her. By deciding to be better, not bitter—as she'd put it—she'd forged a new life for herself. Found the proverbial silver lining.

But she came with baggage. All wrapped up in a four-point-eight-pound bundle of blue eyes and blond hair. Yes, Grace was cute as a button. But she was also the child of violence and trauma.

A cloud scuttled across the sun, dimming the bright sunlight for a moment, and a chill rippled through him. He wished he could get past that, as Kelsey had. In that first, brief connection with her daughter, when Grace had taken her finger and looked into her eyes, any doubts she'd harbored about her ability to love without reservation seemed to have evaporated.

But since his hadn't, he didn't see how Hannah's romantic dreams had any chance of ever becoming anything more than fantasy.

Chapter Fifteen

Pausing outside Kelsey's door, Luke shifted the bouquet of pink roses, baby's breath and fern from one hand to the other.

This was a mistake.

If he couldn't deal with Kelsey's baby, he should keep his distance, not bring her flowers—and lead her on. Yes, he wanted to check on her, confirm she was okay. But he could have accomplished that with a phone call.

Maybe he'd just leave the roses at the nurses' station and ask one of them to—

"Luke?"

Too late. Kelsey's greeting came from behind him, in the hall.

He took a deep breath. Summoned up a smile. Turned.

And froze.

Gone was the woman whose face had been contorted with pain while she shivered and shook in his arms less than thirty-six hours ago. Today, Kelsey was radiant, glowing—and gorgeous.

"Hi. I didn't expect to see you." She searched his eyes, as if looking for a change of heart he couldn't offer, then gestured to the flowers. "And I certainly didn't expect those."

He cleared his throat, praying his voice wouldn't come out in a squeak. "You earned them. You were a real trouper Saturday night."

"It was worth it." She reached out and fingered a petal. "The nurse told me you called last night. Sorry I missed you. I was in the nursery, trying to feed Grace."

"How is she?"

It was a perfunctory, polite question—nothing more—and some subtle nuance in her demeanor told him she knew that.

"The neonatal specialist wants to keep her for a few days, but her early arrival didn't seem to cause any problems other than low birth weight. The biggest worry at the moment is getting her to breastfeed. They're concerned she doesn't yet have the coordination to suck and swallow."

"That can happen with preemies. She'll pick it up."

"Would you like to come in?" She indicated the room behind him. "Hannah called and told me the fantastic news last night. I've been thinking through some publicity ideas I'd like to share with you."

"Are you certain you're up to that?"

She gave him a steady look. "I don't renege on commitments, Luke. Just because I had a baby doesn't mean I'm going to drop the ball on the youth center project. I know how to juggle multiple duties and obligations." She held his gaze for a few seconds, then lifted one shoulder and lightened her voice. "Besides, I need a diversion. I'm not used to sitting around all day doing nothing."

"You could use a little downtime after all that's happened in the past day and a half. But if you're sure, I'll stay for a minute. I'm on my way to a special board meeting at St. Francis, to discuss the latest development, and this way I can pass on your thoughts as well."

He stepped aside to allow her to enter, setting the flowers on her nightstand after following her in. She eased gingerly onto the side of the bed as he took the chair.

"Why don't you start? Any updates since last night?" She shifted, as if trying to get comfortable.

"Yes. I called our Grammy winner, and she not only agreed to come, she donated two pairs of concert tickets and a backstage tour to the auction. She also solicited some of her celebrity friends to donate autographed personal items."

Luke ticked off a few names, and Kelsey's eyebrows rose.

"That's impressive. And it makes my job even easier. Let me run you through some of the publicity ideas I've already jotted down."

Reaching over to the nightstand, she picked up a piece of paper filled with bullet points and briefed him. When she finished, she lowered the sheet to her lap.

"You know, the support of a name entertainer gives us a great opportunity to not only meet, but exceed, your goal. This is exactly what the dinner auction needed in order to garner big bucks and national media attention. If we milk this opportunity for all it's worth, we might be able to raise not just enough money to build the center, but to create an endowment that could fund operating expenses for years to come. Wouldn't that be fabulous?"

Her eyes were shining at the prospect, her face luminous, and Luke had difficulty focusing on her words. Only in its absence did he recognize the tension that had sharpened her features for all the weeks he'd known her. The new, subtle softening enhanced her already considerable beauty.

With an effort, he pulled himself back to the conversation. She'd made a comment that needed a response—something about establishing an endowment.

"Yeah. That would be wonderful. And you can take a lot of the credit for our success. I might have been able to get the ball rolling without you, but I wouldn't have scored a home run."

A soft flush suffused her cheeks, and she leaned over to set her notes back on the nightstand. As she did so, her hospital gown slipped down her shoulder, revealing the ragged scar near her collarbone. Luke stared at it until she hitched the gown back into place with a firm tug.

"That's part of me, too, Luke. And it's not going away, either."

At her quiet comment, he lifted his gaze. Try as he might, he couldn't come up with a response.

Some of the light in her eyes dimmed as she tucked her blond hair behind her ear and folded her hands in her lap.

"I know you were blindsided the other night, when I told you my story. And I understand that. I also know you were probably shocked when I made my decision on the spot after Grace was born. But I'd been praying for guidance, and God gave it to me the instant I looked into my daughter's eyes."

She leaned forward, her posture intent. "Here's the thing, Luke. Because of Grace, my life was transformed. Not in the manner I would have chosen, but the end result has been good. I thought I'd sacrificed the dream of a family to my career. Now I have one. I carried Grace near my heart for eight months, and in that time she claimed a part of it. I love her for who and what she is—a gift of grace from God. And I can't give her up. She needs me and I need her. However…there's room for more people in our circle of love."

Luke had already figured out that Kelsey and Grace were a package deal. Hearing it put into words, though, left an empty feeling in the pit of his stomach. Especially now that she'd made it clear she was interested in exploring *their* relationship.

But he needed to repay honesty with honesty.

"I wish I could say your choice doesn't make any difference to us, Kelsey. But it does. This scar…" he brushed his fingers over the cotton fabric at her collarbone that covered the jagged line "…will always be a reminder of what happened. But scars fade. A child grows. Grace will always be present, a vivid reminder of violence. She's part of you, yes, but part of him, too. And she's part of an incident that feels like a punch in the gut every time I think about it. I'm not sure I can get past that."

A resigned sadness dulled the vibrant green of her irises. "I'm sorry, Luke. For all of us." She swallowed, and though her eyes were shimmering, she managed a shaky smile. "Let me know how the meeting goes, okay? In the meantime, I'll start making some media contacts."

The subject was closed. She'd taken her stand, and she wasn't backing down. Luke admired that, even if he suddenly felt more alone than he ever had in his life.

He stood and moved to the end of the bed. The sun coming in the large window highlighted the high cheekbones and firm chin that imbued her face with strength. He'd met a lot of brave men and women in his line of work, but Kelsey ranked up there with the best of them. Her actions over the past eight months demonstrated that—as did her decision to keep Grace even at the risk of losing a chance at love.

He didn't know if he would have been as strong—and selfless—in her place.

"Well…I guess I'll head out. How long will you be here?"

"Dr. Evans plans to spring me tomorrow. Dorothy said she'd pick me up." She waited, as if hoping he might offer to take her home instead.

He didn't.

"Okay." He tried to ignore the flicker of pain in her eyes. "I'll let you know what happens at the board meeting."

"Good." She averted her head and gestured toward the flowers. "Thank you again for these."

He couldn't see her face now, but he detected tears in her voice. "It was my pleasure."

"I'll talk to you soon." She shifted away from him and arranged the pillow. Waiting for him to leave.

So he did.

But instead of heading for the exit, he found himself walking toward the nursery. Grace was easy to spot through the large window. She was still in the enclosed crib, several monitors stuck to her chest, still wearing the pink cap. Now that her hair was dry, the fine gold ringlets peeking out were the same shade as her mom's.

As if sensing his presence, she turned her head in his direction, stuck her thumb in her mouth and gave him a solemn look. As if to say, "Why don't you like me?"

And that was the problem. He didn't dislike this innocent little infant. He disliked what she represented. Even looking at her now, his thoughts were on Kelsey, on all she'd endured at the hands of her attacker. And once more fury began to churn in his gut.

As she watched him, Grace's face puckered and grew red. Kicking her tiny legs and flailing her arms, she began to cry—almost as if she'd read his expression or sensed his mood. Which only reinforced his conviction that trying to play the role of father to this infant would not be in her best interest.

One of the nurses moved beside her, blocking his view, and he took that as his cue to leave. No noise followed him down the hall from the soundproof nursery, but he knew Grace was sobbing her heart out. That she wanted the comfort of Kelsey's arms.

He could relate.

Two hours later, as Grace finally got the hang of breast-feeding, Kelsey let out a relieved sigh. Smiling down at the infant nestled against her, she cuddled her close. That was one piece of good news today, anyway.

"That's Mommy's good girl," she whispered, touching one of her daughter's ringlets, the hair so fine it was like the whisper of an angel against her fingers. "Now your little tummy will be full. And I'll never let it be empty again."

Grace watched her, those big, blue eyes filled with innocence and absolute trust as they claimed yet another chunk of real estate in Kelsey's heart.

Too bad Luke was immune to their charms.

Kelsey had known, when she'd set the ground rules earlier, that the package deal stipulation could be a deal breaker. But painful as it was to give up the possibility of a future with Luke, letting go of her daughter wasn't an option. Not anymore.

"It looks like she's making up for lost time."

At the nurse's comment, Kelsey blinked away her tears and raised her head. "I think she was *very* hungry."

The nurse tipped her head. "Are you having some pain?"

"No." Not with the breast-feeding. Her heart was another story. "I'm fine. Just a little emotional."

"That can happen with new mothers." The nurse smiled and tucked the blanket around Grace. "Too many hormones running wild. But things will settle down soon, and you'll feel more like yourself."

The nurse moved on, and Kelsey thought about her comment. Who was Kelsey Anderson these days, anyway? The career-focused Kelsey she'd known a year ago didn't exist anymore. The pregnant Kelsey agonizing over her options was gone. The romantic Kelsey who'd begun to think that maybe—just maybe—she might be destined to share her tomorrows with a handsome army doctor had also vanished.

So who was left?

Grace grabbed her gown and tugged—giving her an answer.

Kelsey the mom was left. Kelsey the independent business owner was left. Kelsey the woman of faith was left.

And with or without Luke, that woman would endure.

But she'd much prefer that it be *with* Luke.

As Luke swung into his driveway, he glanced at Kelsey's cottage through the trees. She'd come home two days ago as planned, but other than some lights through the trees at night, he hadn't seen any sign of her. Not that he'd been around much. Since the news of their special guest star and celebrity auction items had hit, he'd been racing around at full throttle, doing a whole new round of interviews Kelsey had arranged and meeting with the manager at the hotel where the event was being held. They'd had to move the dinner to the grand ballroom to accommodate the surge in ticket requests.

He slid out of the car and shut the door. Started toward his house. Hesitated.

Although he'd talked to Kelsey by phone over the past three days, discussing details about promotional opportunities, he hadn't seen her. And he wanted to.

But seeking her out wasn't a good idea. Not in light of the line she'd drawn in the sand during their last face-to-face encounter. No matter how appealing he found her, Grace was a stumbling block. Period. They were at an impasse.

Forcing himself to turn away from the cottage, he headed for his own house and the solitary dinner that awaited him.

Easy to assemble.

Ha!

Kelsey huffed out a frustrated breath as she reread the bold heading on the instructions and surveyed the pieces of the crib she'd purchased this afternoon, spread around the floor of her living room.

It would take an engineer to put this thing together. And where was the packet of screws that was supposed to be included?

She had half a mind to shove the whole thing back into its box and haul it back to the store in Holland where she'd bought it.

Except the end of the box was ripped to shreds. The crib had been a lot heavier than she'd expected, and she'd ended up having to drag it across the gravel drive to get it in the house. A stunt she knew Dr. Evans wouldn't have sanctioned. Driving was one thing. Heavy lifting was another.

But how else was she supposed to get it inside? She didn't have anyone to help her.

As she stared at the instructions in her hands, the

print blurred and she swiped at her eyes to clear her vision. A wayward tear escaped, though, plopping onto the paper and smudging the type. Now it was hard to decipher.

Kind of like her life.

Okay, Kelsey, take a deep breath. You're tired from all the trips to the hospital to see Grace. You're frustrated. You're still healing. Give yourself a break. You'll get this put together. You don't need it until Sunday at the earliest. That's three days. Things will work out. You'll feel better after your hormones settle down.

The little pep talk helped. So did the deep breathing. The left side of her brain kicked in again. Maybe the screws had fallen out the bottom of the box as she'd dragged it from the car to the house. It was worth a look, anyway.

Using the sofa to steady herself, she rose, still a bit off-balance by her lighter weight. She had a ways to go to fit into her pre-pregnancy clothes, but at the rate her body was returning to normal, she'd be there a lot faster than she'd expected. That was one positive.

After one more survey of the mess on her living room floor to confirm that the packet of screws was, indeed, missing, she headed for the back door. She was a smart woman. She had an eye for design and how things fit together. So she'd find the screws. Start fresh on the crib. And she *would* get it put together!

* * *

From his seat on the deck, Luke caught a movement next door through the trees.

Kelsey.

He sat up straighter, watching her walk down the driveway toward her car, her attention fixed on the ground in front of her, as if she was looking for something. When she reached the car, she got down on her hands and knees and peered underneath.

What was going on?

Luke set his soft drink on the table and rose, his barely touched microwave dinner forgotten. Kelsey should be resting, not performing gymnastics. Why wasn't her sister doing whatever it was that needed doing?

Or maybe her sister hadn't yet made it into town.

He'd asked about her arrival in one of their phone conversations, but Kelsey had sidestepped the question. Meaning she might be alone. And in need of help. Not that she was likely to ask for any, in light of their last conversation at the hospital. But just because there might not be a romantic future for them didn't mean he couldn't be a good neighbor.

Decision made, he strode across the lawn and cut through the woods, emerging a few feet away from Kelsey. "Is everything okay?"

At his question, she jerked and turned startled eyes toward him, listing to one side as she lost her balance.

He was beside her in a heartbeat, grabbing her arms to steady her. "Sorry. I saw you through the trees. It looked like you were searching for something. Here, let me help you up." He extended his hand.

She took it, and he gently drew her to her feet.

"I thought I might have dropped a pack of screws. But I don't see them anywhere." She scanned the ground again.

"What do you need with a pack of screws?"

"They're for the crib I'm putting together." She took a few steps toward the back of the car. "I think they forgot to put them in the box."

"You're putting a crib together? By yourself?"

"Yes." She gave a rueful shrug. "Or trying to. The box said it was easy to assemble. What a joke—even if I did have all the parts."

He frowned. "You carried a heavy crib into the house by yourself?"

She bit her lower lip and went into search mode again, turning away from him. "It was no big deal."

"Didn't your doctor tell you not to do any heavy lifting for at least two weeks?"

"It wasn't heavy, just awkward. And I didn't lift. I dragged. They put it in the car for me at the store."

"Why didn't your sister help you?"

Hand on the trunk, she swiveled toward him. "She's not coming. She and two of her kids have the flu. The bad, full-blown kind. She won't be able to get away for two or three weeks, and by then I won't need her."

Luke propped a fist on his hip and raked his fingers through his hair. "I live next door, Kelsey. Why didn't you ask me for help?"

She rubbed a finger down the seam in the trunk. "You're busy with the youth center project. I didn't want to bother you."

He regarded her for a moment, then closed the distance between them until he stood inches away. She seemed taken aback by his move, but held her ground as he locked gazes with her.

"It's too late for you to worry about bothering me." He let that comment sink in before he continued. "However, I don't mind being bothered with practical problems. Come on, show me the crib and we'll see if we can get it assembled."

There was no way he was taking no for an answer. Up close, Kelsey looked too pale for his liking, and there were lines of fatigue around her mouth and at the corners of her eyes. All of which told him she'd been pushing herself too hard and that she needed help. Whether she wanted to admit it or not.

To his relief, she didn't balk at his offer.

"Okay. I know I'd figure it out eventually on my own, but two heads may be better than one. If we can find the missing screws."

An hour and a half later, after they'd located the screws and he'd appropriated the hands-on role—delegating her to reading the instructions and finding the needed parts—he leaned back on his heels and examined the result of their labor.

"It looks good, doesn't it?" Kelsey ran a hand over the pristine white crib, letting her fingers linger on the whimsical fairies that decorated the edge of the headboard.

"Very nice." Luke rose. "Where do you want it?"

"In the first guest room. I'm going to take down the bed that's in there, but for now I can put the crib along the inside wall."

She moved to one side, as if to help, but he shook his head. "I can handle it. Remember—no heavy lifting."

"Fine."

She preceded him into the hall and flipped on the light. After picking up the crib, he followed her to the bedroom and set it beside the wall in the spot she indicated.

"Perfect. Thank you."

"My pleasure. Do you want me to take the bed down for you?" He gestured toward the double bed.

"Not tonight. Thanks."

"Whenever you're ready, let me know."

She gave him a shaky smile. "I better do it quick, then. You'll be leaving in twelve days. The Tuesday after the benefit, right?"

"Right." He shoved his hands in his pockets and

propped a shoulder against the wall. "You'll have the beach all to yourself again."

"How come that isn't as appealing as it once was?"

Her words were soft, and as he watched, a tear spilled onto her cheek.

She swiped it away and made a move to brush past him. "Sorry. My hormones are wacky. I get emotional over everything."

"My hormones are fine." He reached for her as she passed, taking her arms in a gentle grasp as he pulled her close. "But I get emotional when I think about leaving, too."

He heard her breath hitch in her throat, and her eyes filled with a yearning that set his pulse racing. That made him want to hold her close and promise he'd always be her rock. That made him want to taste her soft, slightly parted lips.

Had she tugged free, Luke would have resisted the temptation to kiss her. And she had every opportunity to do that as they looked at each other in the quiet house that had long been her refuge.

But she didn't. And he couldn't ignore the message—the invitation—in her eyes.

Cupping her cheek with one hand, he stroked her silky blond hair with the other. Traced the elegant curve of her jaw with a finger that wasn't quite steady. Inhaled the faint flowery fragrance that was all Kelsey.

And then, bending down, he claimed her lips.

Luke had intended to keep his kiss gentle, scarching, exploratory. But when Kelsey melted against him and her arms went around his neck, all his good intentions scattered. The kiss deepened as they both gave in to the feelings they'd been holding inside for weeks.

In the end, it was Luke, not Kelsey, who broke contact. Not because he wanted to, but because he had to. Things were getting way too intense.

She rested her forehead against his chest, and he held her in the circle of his arms until at last she backed up enough to look up at him. "I didn't expect that."

"I didn't, either."

She searched his face. "It doesn't change anything, though, does it?"

"For me or for you?"

"I can't give up Grace, Luke."

"I know. But she's not the only problem."

She stiffened in his arms. "She isn't a problem, Luke. She's a person."

Way to go, Turner.

"I realize that. I'm sorry. But there are other issues. Like geography. I have a job waiting for me in Atlanta. Your life is here."

She played with a button on his shirt, and he had to force himself to concentrate on her words.

"I love Gram's cottage. It will always be my refuge. But my work is mobile. Most of my business comes from my website anyway, and if I do design a line of quilted items, those will be mass-produced elsewhere. Besides, I think my shop mate may soon retire. Dorothy and Charles are getting serious, and I wouldn't be surprised if there's a wedding in the not too distant future. If that happened, I'd close my shop and work from home."

So Hannah had been right. Kelsey wasn't married to Michigan. That was good news.

She lifted her chin, and her hand stilled as she continued. "And home could be anywhere. As long as I'm with the people I love."

Including Grace.

They were back to square one.

Yet he didn't want to lose this woman. She belonged here, in his arms. He was becoming more and more certain of that with every passing day.

"Maybe we could give this some time, Kelsey. I might be able to work through my issues with Grace."

She let out a long sigh. "I guess it's unrealistic to expect you to welcome her with open arms, since I had no idea how *I* would react to her when she was born." Then her spine stiffened, and her expression grew fierce. "But I don't want you to accept Grace just to get me. I would never, ever want her to think she was excess baggage."

Luke wished his willingness to consider accepting Grace had a nobler motive. But Kelsey had him pegged. He was wavering because he wanted *her*—not her daughter—in his arms.

And Kelsey seemed to intuit that. Slowly disengaging from his embrace, she stepped back and crossed her arms over her chest.

"I wish things were different, Luke."

He shoved his hands in his pockets. "So do I."

"Well…thanks again for helping with the crib." She edged past him and led the way to the back door, leaving him no choice but to follow.

When she pushed it open for him, he caught the glimmer of tears in her eyes, and he took an involuntary step toward her.

She jerked back and shook her head, angling away from him. "Don't."

At her choked plea, he checked himself. He'd made one mistake already, with the kiss. He didn't want to compound it. "I'll talk to you this week—about the benefit."

She gave a stiff nod.

As he exited through the screened porch, he heard the door close behind him.

And Luke had a sick feeling in the pit of his stomach that she was closing the door not just on her house, but on her heart.

Chapter Sixteen

At the sound of the doorbell, Kelsey shifted Grace onto her shoulder and gently began to pat her back as she headed toward the front of the house.

"Come on, sweetie. Burp for me, okay? Please?"

That pleading refrain had been Kelsey's mantra in the two days since she'd brought her daughter home. The sweet, compliant little bundle of joy in the hospital nursery had morphed into a fussy, unhappy baby who didn't want to eat, sleep or poop, let alone burp.

A call to the help line at the birth center had reassured her Grace's fussiness and irritability were normal, that she just needed time to adjust to her new environment. But it was nerve-wracking. At only an ounce over five pounds, Grace couldn't afford not to eat.

The bell rang again and she picked up her pace, irritated.

She did *not* need a visitor.

But when she found Reverend Howard on her doorstep, holding a basket of flowers with balloons attached, a small, stuffed animal with a bow around its neck tucked under his arm, she relented. After all the hours she'd spent bending his ear as she agonized over her decision, she owed him more than the quick call she'd made after Grace's birth to inform him she was keeping her baby.

"Is this a good time?" He eyed the bundle on her shoulder. "Tell me if it's not and I'll leave these things and stop in some other day."

"To be honest, no time has been good recently."

As if to verify that point, Grace spit up on her shoulder. Kelsey felt the dampness seep through the towel.

"I'll come back."

The minister started to set his gifts inside the front door, but Kelsey stepped back and motioned him in. "No, please stay. I could use a distraction for a few minutes. Let me just get rid of this towel."

She ushered him into the living room and gestured toward the sofa. "Have a seat. I'll be right back."

A quick detour to the improvised nursery took care of the towel, but her attempts to put Grace in her crib were met with howls of protest. Kelsey sighed. No way could she ignore her child's distress—as Grace had already learned. She picked her up again, bouncing her slightly in her arms as she rejoined the minister and took a seat on the couch beside him.

He leaned close for a look, and Kelsey folded back the blanket. The baby stared up at him and hiccupped.

"She's a cutie."

"Thank you. She also has a good set of lungs."

"Not getting much sleep, I assume?"

"Not enough." She picked up the stuffed animal the minister had set on the coffee table and tucked it next to Grace. "Thank you for this and the flowers."

"My pleasure. Celebrating the miracle of birth is always a joy. Other than not getting much sleep, how are you feeling?"

"Physically, okay. Emotionally, at peace." She stroked a finger down Grace's satin-smooth cheek, giving her a tender smile as the baby grabbed it.

"I can see that. I'm happy for you."

"I kept meaning to call you back and talk more. But things have been hectic."

"So I heard. I thought you might be up to attending services Sunday, but Luke told me afterward that Grace was coming home that day. I imagine you've had your hands full."

"That would be an understatement."

"Luke also filled me in on all the publicity work you've been doing since our celebrity guest agreed to come to the benefit. He's very grateful. We all are."

"It's a worthy cause. Carlos sounded like he was a man worth honoring."

"I know his friendship meant a lot to Luke. As a matter of fact, so does yours."

Grace emitted a soft sigh and burrowed deeper into the blanket, giving Kelsey an excuse to look down. "He's a very special man."

"Who thinks you're very special as well."

Kelsey swallowed past the sudden tightness in her throat. "But he doesn't think that about Grace."

"He has nothing against Grace, Kelsey. He recognizes that she's an innocent party in this whole situation, and that she's a child of God. But he has concerns about his ability to love her as she deserves to be loved."

"I'm not willing to settle for anything less."

"He knows that. That's why he's struggling."

"Loving someone shouldn't have to be a struggle."

"Ah, my dear." The hint of a smile touched the minister's lips. "Loving people is *often* a struggle in our imperfect world. The important thing is to keep trying with a sincere heart. And he is trying."

Kelsey creased the edge of Grace's blanket between her fingers. "Did he ask you to talk to me?"

"No. But I've come to admire him a great deal these past weeks. And you, over the past few months. I can't help but feel God brought the two of you together for a reason."

"Maybe it was simply to give Carlos's dream wings."

"Perhaps. Then again, He may have had somethin more in mind. Many blessings come in unexpecte ways, as you well know. That's why it's importan for us to be open to the opportunities He sends ou way." The man rose, rested a gentle hand on Grace' head and moved to the door. "I'll let myself out. Ca if you need anything."

Long after the door closed behind him, Kelse remained on the couch, Grace's rosebud lips suck ling in sleep, her countenance peaceful. Alread Kelsey loved her more than life itself.

Was it possible, given time, Luke could feel th same way?

She thought back to the story he'd told her abou the roadside bomb, and how he'd barricaded h heart afterward in order to survive. Initially, he resisted Carlos's efforts to break through thos walls. Had considered the man a pest. Yet Carl had triumphed in the end. With his solid faith, pe sistence and positive outlook, the young medic ha won Luke's respect, friendship and love.

Could Grace's innocent sweetness work the san magic in his heart, over time?

As she settled back into the corner of the couc her baby tucked close, Kelsey's eyelids grew heav Should she risk a romance with Luke and pray he come to love Grace as she did? Or was she doing disservice to all of them by holding out hope for fairy-tale ending?

Kelsey had no idea. But as she hovered in th

ethereal state between slumber and wakefulness, she sent a silent plea to the One who did.

Lord, please show me the way.

Sliding into his car as the bells at St. Francis chimed the midnight hour several blocks away, Luke loosened his bow tie and took a deep breath.

The dinner auction had been a resounding success. The hotel ballroom had been packed, every auction item had sold at an amazing price, and his talk about Carlos had been met with a standing ovation. Best of all, they'd raised every dollar needed to not only build the youth center, but fund an endowment, as Kelsey had predicted.

Too bad she couldn't have been there to witness the fruits of her labors.

Luke turned the key in the ignition, backed out of the parking spot and headed toward Pier Cove, his thoughts on Kelsey. Her absence had been the only flaw in the evening. They'd made plans weeks ago to attend together, but with Grace home from the hospital for just six days, she hadn't wanted to leave her. He understood.

But he'd missed her.

In fact, he'd been missing her all week, despite the daily phone calls he made from his cell as he ran to meetings and interviews, dealt with their special guest star and finalized banquet arrangements. Twice he'd stopped by when he'd been home during the day, but that had been a mistake. Both times he'd awakened her, and she'd met him at the door bleary-eyed and sleepy. In light of the dark circles under her eyes and the lines of fatigue on her face, he hadn't wanted to risk interrupting her much-needed rest again.

Still, having her by his side tonight would have been the proverbial icing on the cake. They could have celebrated the moment together.

As he covered the dark miles between Saugatuck and Pier Cove, Luke thought about the ovation he'd received tonight as he'd spoken of the young medic who had inspired him, and whose memory the youth center would honor. And he hoped Carlos somehow knew his dream would become a reality. That thanks to him, other teens would have the chance to turn their lives around, just as he had.

Now, his mission completed, he could go home. And move on with his life.

Except the thought of doing that without Kelsey left a hollow feeling in the pit of his stomach.

Exiting I-196 at Pier Cove, he drove down the narrow, woodsy road that paralleled the shore, anxious to get home. The only thing on his agenda for the next two days was a meeting with the Interdenominational Youth Fellowship board to wrap things up and talk about the role he'd play as an advisory board member until the center was completed. That left him plenty of time to focus on Kelsey—his top priority.

There was no way he could walk away from her

in three days with no hope of ever seeing her again. He had to convince her to give him a chance to learn to love Grace.

Luke wasn't certain he could get past the trauma of her conception and the bad feelings it invoked. But he'd been praying about it, and he hoped, with God's grace, he could manage it.

Because if he couldn't, there was no future for him and Kelsey. It wouldn't be fair to any of them.

The headlights picked out his driveway ahead, and he swung in, glancing at Kelsey's house through the trees. As he'd discovered during his stay, she left lights on at night. A lot of lights. Considering what she'd been through, her aversion to darkness and shadows didn't surprise him.

But tonight there were far more lights on than usual.

As he braked to a stop and slid out of the car, the faint wail of a baby floated through the cool night air.

If Grace was awake, so was Kelsey.

Luke was tempted to cut through the trees and knock on her door. But it was the middle of the night, and while she might be awake, she was probably not in the mood for visitors. A recap of the evening could wait until a decent hour.

He was starting to turn away when he heard a crash from Kelsey's cottage. The baby's wails increased in volume.

Following his instincts, he switched direction and

strode through the trees toward her back door. From the screen porch, he caught a glimpse of her through the kitchen window. The counter was littered with broken crockery, the baby was wailing in her arms and tears were running down her cheeks.

He moved to the back door, calling through the window as he knocked. "Kelsey, it's Luke."

At the sound, she swung toward him, then stumbled toward the door. He heard a startled exclamation as he lost sight of her, and a moment later the locks were flipped. The door was pulled open. Then Kelsey stood before him, still bouncing Grace on her shoulder.

She was a mess.

Her hair was tangled, there were bruise-like shadows under her eyes, her T-shirt was stained and she was trembling.

"What's going on? I heard the crash as I pulled in."

"I was up anyway, so I thought I'd empty the d-dishwasher. The plates slipped when I tried to s-slide them in the cabinet."

In one sweep, Luke took in the scene behind her. It looked as if several plates had shattered on the countertop and floor. There was also a trail of blood leading across the floor to her foot.

His adrenaline surging, he reached for the baby. "You're hurt." The infant scrunched Kelsey's T-shirt in her fists, and Luke had to pry them free. Settling the squirming, kicking, screaming bundle against his chest, he motioned Kelsey toward a kitchen chair, away from the mess on the floor. "Sit down and let me see your foot."

With a distressed look at her howling daughter, she limped over to the chair.

Once she was settled, Luke handed Grace back, dropped to one knee and picked up Kelsey's bare foot. The inch-long gash on the bottom was jagged but not deep enough to need stitches. Setting her foot on an adjacent chair, he rose. "Where's your first aid kit?"

"In the hall closet. Where the ice pack was."

He found it in thirty seconds. After cleaning the cut and bandaging it, he closed the box and motioned toward the baby, who continued to cry. "Does she need to be fed or changed?"

"I just finished both."

"Good." He tugged his tie free from his collar, slipped off his jacket and plucked Grace from her arms again. "You need to get some sleep."

"Every time I try to put her down, she cries."

"Babies are very good at training their parents that way." He flashed her a quick grin. "But I'll hold her until she settles down. And I'll stick around for a while, so you can get at least a couple of hours of sleep."

He could tell she was tempted. But he also saw the flash of guilt in her eyes.

"I'm not tired, Kelsey. I'm still on a high from the dinner. You won't believe how much we raised."

When he told her the amount, her mouth dropped open. "Add that to all the individual and corporate contributions that have come in over the past few weeks, and we not only have our center, we have the endowment fund you hoped for."

A smile of delight chased away her fatigue. "That's fabulous, Luke."

"We'll talk more tomorrow. Now go get some sleep."

"Are you sure?"

"Go." He waved her toward the bedroom. "I'll keep this little lady company."

"Okay. Thank you."

She was limping down the hall before he could reply.

Once she disappeared, Luke moved into the living room. Grace continued to flail in his arm, and he bounced her gently as he settled into a rocking chair with a colorful quilt draped over the back.

"How about letting your mom get some sleep, hmm? Can you do that?"

To his surprise, she snuffled and quieted as she regarded him, blue eyes swimming in tears, blond ringlets framing her cherubic face, tiny fists clenched around a pink blanket. She *was* cute. And now that he was up close and personal with her, he could see the features she shared with her mom. The hair was an obvious connection. But she had Kelsey's jaw, too. Strong, with a hint of stubbornness. And her mouth—definitely the same shape as her mother's.

Grace raised her arms toward him, never breaking eye contact, and without thinking, he lifted her to his shoulder, his hand supporting her back. She rested her head against him and snuggled close, and he heard her emit a tiny sigh as she relaxed in his arms.

When had he last held a baby? Luke couldn't remember. Medical school, maybe. He'd forgotten how soft and fragile and vulnerable they felt.

As he continued to rock, he stroked Grace's back. He could feel the beat of her heart as she burrowed deeper against his shoulder. As if she belonged there. As if he were her father. For her, it was simple.

And maybe it could be for him, too. Maybe instead of thinking about how she came to be when he looked at her, he needed to think about the precious gift of life she represented—and the sweet, innocent love she so willingly offered.

A love that was his for the taking. From a child who could be his daughter.

Her tiny hand worked its way across his chest toward his heart, and a rush of tenderness stole his breath and tightened his throat.

And suddenly he *felt* like a father.

Even as the feeling jolted him, he realized it made sense. Because fatherhood wasn't just about genetics and biology. It was also about love. More importantly about love.

As for the past—perhaps he should leave it there. When he looked at Grace in the future, why not think of the joy she'd brought Kelsey? And give thanks to God that He'd showered them with the grace to turn tragedy into triumph and recognize the blessing He'd sent their way?

In a sudden, blinding flash of insight, Luke knew this was the attitude he should take. And if he did, they could make this work. *He* could make this work.

Buoyed by a new optimism, Luke settled back into the chair as Grace slept against his shoulder.

And in the silent early morning hours, he prayed Kelsey would give him a chance to prove he could be a worthy husband and the father Grace deserved.

It was time to feed Grace.

Blinking past the drugged sleep that had sucked her into a black hole for the past…Kelsey peered at the clock on her nightstand…three hours, she swung her feet to the floor and stood.

Strange that Grace wasn't fussing by now. She had to be hungry.

Still trying to shake off her heavy slumber, Kelsey padded down the hall to the nursery—and found an empty crib.

Her pulse skittered, chasing away the last remnants of sleep, and for one terrifying instant she panicked.

Then she remembered. Luke had offered to watch Grace while she grabbed a few hours of sleep.

Favoring her injured foot as she made her way down the hall, she passed the mess on the kitchen floor and paused at the entrance to the living room.

The scene melted her heart.

Near as she could tell, they were both out cold. Luke was half-sitting, half-lying on the couch, his broad shoulders wedged into the corner as he held Grace against his shoulder, his large hand cradling her tiny head against his pristine white tux shirt, her soft golden ringlets peeking through his long, lean fingers.

They looked as if they belonged together.

A wave of melancholy swept over her, but she tamped it down as she moved beside them and touched his shoulder. It was foolish to wish for something that would probably never be.

"Luke…" She spoke in a whisper, keeping tabs on her daughter. "I need to feed Grace."

His eyes flickered open. For a moment he seemed disoriented. Then he carefully straightened up, keeping Grace cradled in his arms.

Puckering her mouth, Grace blinked and focused on Luke. He smiled at her…and Kelsey could have sworn her daughter smiled back. But that was silly. Babies this age didn't smile. It must be gas.

"Chow time, Grace." He touched the infant's cheek with his finger.

The baby gurgled.

Kelsey reached for her, but even though her daughter had to be hungry, she clung to Luke's shirt.

"Looks like you've made a friend."

Grinning, Luke disengaged her fingers with a gentle tug and handed her over. "Yeah. It's mutual. She and I have come to an understanding, right, sweetie?"

Sweetie?

"Have I missed something here?" Kelsey shot him a cautious glance.

"You have. And I'll fill you in while you feed her."

An ember of hope sparked to life in Kelsey. "Are you sure you don't want to wait until tomorrow? It's almost four o'clock. You must be tired."

"This can't wait."

The spark ignited. "Okay. Let me grab a blanket."

Kelsey retraced her steps to the nursery, snatched one off the bed and rejoined Luke. He patted the cushion beside him, and she sat.

Anxious to hear what he had to say, she draped the blanket over her shoulder, got Grace started, and turned to him. "So what couldn't wait?"

His eyes warmed and deepened in color. "This." Leaning close, he brushed his lips over hers.

Kelsey's heart stopped. Raced on.

When he backed off she stared at him, willing her lungs to kick in again. "Wh-what was that for?"

"To let you know I'm falling in love with you. And with Grace."

She closed her eyes. *Lord, is this for real? I want to believe You've answered my prayers, but it seems too easy.*

"Hey." Luke touched her cheek, waiting until she opened her eyes before he continued. "I know what you're thinking. That I'm just saying this because I don't want to let you go. And I don't blame you, after all the fuss I made. But you know what? I've been praying for guidance. And tonight, when I held Grace in my arms, I realized that what counts is the future, not the past. I saw her for what she is—a blessing from God. Without her, you would still be clawing your way up the corporate ladder and we would never have met. When I look at her now, I feel gratitude for the role she played in transforming your life and bringing us together. And I'll give thanks for her every day of my life."

Tears blurred Kelsey's vision as she looked at this man of integrity and honor who'd entered her life in the most unexpected of ways. Whose selflessness and compassion had driven him to keep a promise made to a fallen comrade, and thereby led him into her arms. Whose kindness and caring had helped her heal and find the courage to love.

Reverend Howard had been right. God had indeed envisioned a larger role for them, one that went far beyond simply being neighbors or working together to help a young man realize a dream.

Shifting toward her, Luke put one arm around her shoulders and laid his other hand atop hers, where it rested on Grace.

"Here's what I'd like to propose, Kelsey. We've only known each other a short time. I'm leaving Tuesday. But as Hannah reminded me, distance doesn't have to be a problem. We'll talk often, and I'll come back for frequent visits. Take as long as you need to feel comfortable that my love for Grace is real and that what we have is strong enough to last forever. I'll wait."

He gestured to Gram's wall hanging. "I was looking at that tonight as I rocked Grace. And it reminded me of a comment Hannah made the day she showed me *her* wall hanging. She said you'd smoothed out the rough edges." He turned to her and the love shining in his eyes was as warm as an August day on Pier Cove beach. "You did the same for me, Kelsey. You smoothed out the rough edges of my life. A life that was pretty tattered after ten tough years. And I'd like to spend the rest of it returning the favor. So will you give me a chance to prove I'm worthy of you—and Grace?"

At the mention of her name, Grace batted away the blanket and tipped her head out to peer up at them. Then she reached out her tiny hand and touched their linked fingers.

Luke chuckled. "I think I won *her* over. What about her mom?"

A tear spilled out of Kelsey's eye, even as joy

overflowed in her heart. "I'm not usually a crier, just so you know."

"I'll have to take your word for that."

"It's the hormones."

"I don't care what it is, as long as you're willing to give me a chance."

She smiled and blinked the moisture out of her eyes. "I am absolutely willing to give you a chance. And I'd throw myself in your arms to prove it if I wasn't otherwise occupied."

A slow smile spread over his face, warming her from the tips of her toes to the top of her head. "Hold that thought for later. Right now, I guess this will have to suffice."

He leaned toward her, and as she angled her head for his kiss, she caught sight of Gram's wall hanging.

"Live. Love. Rejoice."

It was good advice.

And she intended to follow it every day of her life.

Epilogue

Four Months Later

Shovels poised, Luke and Father Joe posed as cameras clicked around them and a dozen network and local news teams recorded the groundbreaking ceremony for the Carlos Fernandez Interdenominational Youth Center.

From her spot on the sidelines, Kelsey gave the hood on Grace's snowsuit a little tug and sent Luke a reassuring smile as he looked her way. She knew he was worried about Grace being out in the late-December cold, but her daughter was well bundled up. Besides, with Dorothy preparing to walk down the aisle later this afternoon, the older woman had been unavailable for babysitting duty.

And no way had Kelsey intended to miss this moment.

Once the photographers were satisfied, Luke shook hands with Father Joe and the other board members, then started toward her. He was intercepted several times by reporters, and while he answered their questions graciously, she could tell he was anxious to rejoin her.

No more anxious than she was to have him by her side.

In these past four months, they'd talked every day—often several times a day. Their phone calls had been supplemented with long weekend visits when he'd flown up to see her, once again occupying his friend's house next door.

Now it was her turn to visit him. Tomorrow the three of them would fly to Atlanta so she could meet his parents and spend Christmas with his family.

Meeting the parents was a big step.

One she was ready to take.

For over the past four months, all her concerns had been put to rest as she'd watched Luke interact with Grace. Every tender touch, every gentle smile, every loving cuddle had proven he did, indeed, consider her daughter a blessing.

Coming up beside them, his breath making frosty clouds in the cold air, he adjusted the scarf that covered the bottom half of Grace's face and leaned down to give Kelsey a quick kiss.

"Wow. Cold lips." He reared back with a grin.

"Warm heart."

He winked. "I know. Come on. Let's get you two out of the wind." He ushered them toward her car, settled Grace in her safety seat, and slid behind the wheel. "One down, two to go."

"Two? Is there some other event on our agenda besides Dorothy's wedding?"

"Maybe."

Her heart skipped a beat. "Want to let me in on the secret?"

"Nope."

With that, he pulled into the street and headed back to Pier Cove so they could get ready for the wedding.

Leaving her to wonder what he had up his sleeve.

Two hours later, as Luke climbed the steps to Kelsey's screened porch after freshening up at his friend's house, he fingered the ring in his pocket.

This was the day.

He could have waited until Christmas Eve. Or Christmas. That would have been more traditional. But somehow, it seemed right to propose here, in the place Kelsey had always loved.

He only hoped she was ready.

Because even though he'd told her he'd wait as long as necessary, it was getting harder and harder to leave at the end of every long weekend. He wanted her and Grace with him all the time, not just six days a month.

He knocked again, and a few seconds later she

pulled the door open, checking her watch. "Aren't you early?"

"More like anxious. I was missing my girls." He slipped inside, shut the door behind him and gave her a slow head-to-toe perusal. She'd returned to her pre-pregnancy weight, and although she complained that she'd gained a permanent inch on her waistline, she was still more attractive—and appealing—than any woman he'd ever dated. "Is Grace awake?"

"Yes."

"Want to get her for a minute?"

"Why?"

"I have a surprise."

She gave him an appraising look, then retreated without another word.

As she disappeared down the hall, he moved into the living room and sat on the couch, holding up his arms for Grace and patting the seat beside him when she returned.

"Aren't we pretty today." He smiled at the little cherub in the crook of his elbow, all dressed up in her first Christmas outfit—a red velvet number with a plaid taffeta insert at the bodice and a skirt edged with lace. Kelsey had even added a red velvet headband with a bow. Then he lifted his eyes. "That goes for both of you."

A becoming blush pinkened Kelsey's cheeks as she started to sit.

"Leave room for Grace."

Following his instruction, Kelsey edged over slightly.

He propped Grace on the seat between them. "I want our little lady here for this. Because it wouldn't have happened without her."

Once Grace was settled, he took Kelsey's hand in his and twined his fingers with hers. "Your hands are still cold."

"But my heart's still warm."

Her husky response, and the encouraging spark of anticipation in her eyes, helped calm his unexpected jitters.

With his free hand, he removed a square jeweler's box from the inside pocket of his jacket and set it on the sofa between them. Her eyes widened, and he heard her breath catch.

"Before I make my little speech, tell me if this is too soon. If it is, I'll put this away."

"No." The word came out in a croak, and she tried again. "No. I love you. *We* love you." She gestured toward Grace, her voice stronger now. Firm and sure. "And we know you love us."

His throat constricted, and when he spoke, his own voice had roughened with emotion. "You're making this much easier than I expected."

"Luke." She leaned toward him and put her hand on his shoulder, her glorious green eyes giving him a window to her heart. "Whatever doubts I once had are long gone. We belong together."

Hearing his own conviction put into words gave

him the confidence to open the box and take out the sparkling solitaire on the gold band.

"I bought this in Atlanta, a few days after the benefit dinner. I was hoping that if I had it in hand, things would progress as I hoped. I guess it worked. Along with a lot of prayers."

Between them, Grace was watching the proceedings with a solemn expression, her thumb stuck in her mouth, and he sent her a smile as he dropped to one knee beside the sofa and took the hand of the woman who'd stolen his heart.

"Kelsey, I love you more than I ever thought I could love anyone, and I would be honored to have you as my wife. I promise that I will love, honor and cherish you all the days of my life. Will you marry me?"

Before Kelsey could respond, Grace pulled her finger out of her mouth, grinned at them, and clapped her hands.

They both stared at her.

"She's too young to do that," Luke said.

"I guess she's a woman who knows her mind. And I'll take that as a sign of approval." Turning back to him, Kelsey smiled, too. "On behalf of the two of us, my answer is *yes*."

Luke slipped the ring on her finger, then framed her beautiful face with his hands. If he lived to be a hundred, he would never forget the love shining in her eyes at this moment. Or the sudden, distant strains of "Amazing Grace" that unexpectedly echoed in the recesses of his mind.

Carlos's favorite song.

How appropriate. For though he'd come to this place to honor his friend, he'd been blessed tenfold in return.

And as he claimed Kelsey's sweet lips in a kiss that spoke of love and hope and a bright tomorrow, he sent a silent thank-you heavenward for the gift of grace that had, indeed, led him home.

* * * * *

Dear Reader,

I have always been a passionate believer in the rights of the unborn, the most innocent and vulnerable of all life. This book gave me the opportunity to create a heroine who shares that belief, and whose compassion, principles and conscience compel her to carry to term a child conceived in violence. Although Kelsey finds herself in the kind of situation even many pro-life proponents would say justifies abortion, she firmly believes that two wrongs don't make a right. And out of her courageous decision comes grace and blessings beyond her imagining.

Writing Kelsey's story gave me a renewed appreciation for the difficult choices many of us face in life, whether it be an unexpected pregnancy, end-of-life decisions, or how best to deal with illness, job loss, betrayal and the myriad problems that are the human lot. May her choice inspire and uplift you, and may you, too, be nurtured and graced by God's love as you travel the sometimes rocky road of life.

Please watch for my next Steeple Hill book, coming in the fall of 2011. In the meantime, I invite you to check my website at www.irenehannon.com for more information about my other books.

Irene Hannon

QUESTIONS FOR DISCUSSION

1. Luke comes to Michigan to fulfill a promise to a man who had a tremendous impact on his life. Is there someone in your life who left a lasting impression? What made him or her stand out?

2. Kelsey has made a very courageous choice. Do you agree with her decision to carry the baby to term? Why or why not?

3. What is your position on abortion? Why do you feel the way you do? If you believe it's wrong, is there ever a situation that justifies it? Why or why not? What guidance does the Bible give on this subject?

4. Although Kelsey suffers a terrible trauma, it causes her to reevaluate her life and make some drastic changes—becoming better, not bitter, as she says in the story. Have you ever found yourself in a bad situation that ultimately led you down a better path?

5. After Luke witnesses the deaths of three friends in a suicide bombing, he shuts down emotionally. Is that healthy? How else might a person cope with such a tragedy?

6. Carlos's grandmother was important in the young medic's life. What do you think might have happened to him if she hadn't employed some tough love when he got into trouble as a teen? What does this say about the importance of involved, caring parents or guardians in a young person's life?

7. Luke is taken aback when Kelsey decides to keep her baby, and he backs off. How did you feel about his response?

8. Why do you think Kelsey was drawn to quilting, even in her corporate ladder-climbing days? Do you have a favorite pastime that gives you solace?

9. At one point, Reverend Howard remarks that loving is often a struggle. Do you think this is true? If so, why? What does the Bible teach us about loving?

10. When the story begins, Kelsey is frightened of Luke. Why does she change her mind over time? Cite specific examples from the story to support your answer.

11. Which secondary character in the book did you find most interesting? Why?

12. At the end of the story, Luke is heading off to Atlanta to direct the E.R. at a major medical center. What experiences and personal qualities will serve him well in this job?

13. What qualities in Kelsey made Luke fall in love with her? Do you think they were a good match?

14. In the end, Luke chooses to view Grace as a gift from God rather than a reminder of violence, just as Kelsey chose to be better, not bitter. What does this suggest about the power of choices and the responsibility we bear for our own happiness?

LARGER-PRINT BOOKS!

GET 2 FREE
LARGER-PRINT NOVELS
PLUS 2 FREE
MYSTERY GIFTS

Larger-print novels are now available...

YES! Please send me 2 FREE LARGER-PRINT Love Inspired® novels and my 2 FREE mystery gifts (gifts are worth about $10). After receiving them, if I don't wish to receive any more books, I can return the shipping statement marked "cancel". If I don't cancel, I will receive 6 brand-new novels every month and be billed just $4.74 per book in the U.S. or $5.24 per book in Canada. That's a saving of at least 24% off the cover price. It's quite a bargain! Shipping and handling is just 50¢ per book in the U.S. and 75¢ per book in Canada.* I understand that accepting the 2 free books and gifts places me under no obligation to buy anything. I can always return a shipment and cancel at any time. Even if I never buy another book, the two free books and gifts are mine to keep forever.

122/322 IDN FC79

Name	(PLEASE PRINT)	
Address		Apt. #
City	State/Prov.	Zip/Postal Code

Signature (If under 18, a parent or guardian must sign)

Mail to the **Reader Service:**
IN U.S.A.: P.O. Box 1867, Buffalo, NY 14240-1867
IN CANADA: P.O. Box 609, Fort Erie, Ontario L2A 5X3

Not valid to current subscribers to Love Inspired Larger-Print books.

**Are you a current subscriber to Love Inspired books
and want to receive the larger-print edition?
Call 1-800-873-8635 or visit www.ReaderService.com.**

* Terms and prices subject to change without notice. Prices do not include applicable taxes. Sales tax applicable in N.Y. Canadian residents will be charged applicable taxes. Offer not valid in Quebec. This offer is limited to one order per household. All orders subject to credit approval. Credit or debit balances in a customer's account(s) may be offset by any other outstanding balance owed by or to the customer. Please allow 4 to 6 weeks for delivery. Offer available while quantities last.

Your Privacy—The Reader Service is committed to protecting your privacy. Our Privacy Policy is available online at www.ReaderService.com or upon request from the Reader Service.

We make a portion of our mailing list available to reputable third parties that offer products we believe may interest you. If you prefer that we not exchange your name with third parties, or if you wish to clarify or modify your communication preferences, please visit us at www.ReaderService.com/consumerchoice or write to us at Reader Service Preference Service, P.O. Box 9062, Buffalo, NY 14269. Include your complete name and address.

LILP11

Love Inspired® SUSPENSE

RIVETING INSPIRATIONAL ROMANCE

Watch for our series of edge-
of-your-seat suspense novels.
These contemporary tales
of intrigue and romance
feature Christian characters
facing challenges to their faith...
and their lives!

AVAILABLE IN REGULAR
& LARGER-PRINT FORMATS

For exciting stories that reflect traditional values,
visit:
www.ReaderService.com

Vivian Cothern
Betty Trimble
Pauline Cloud
June Kelley
Fern Fisher